existential TERROR and breakfast
season one

M.P. Fitzgerald

injecting Gonzo into fiction

Seattle

EXISTENTIAL TERROR AND BREAKFAST: SEASON ONE
By M.P. Fitzgerald

This is a work of fiction, Names, characters, places, and incidents either are tho product of the author's imagination or are used fictitiously. Any resemblance to actual persons, living or dead, events, or locales is entirely coincidental.

Copyright © by M.P. Fitzgerald

All rights reserved.

This book or any portion thereof may not be reproduced or used in any manner whatsoever without the express written permission of the author except for the use of brief quotations in a book review.

Printed in the United States of America

First printing, 2018

M.P. Fitzgerald

420 Wall St. #216

Seattle, WA 98121

https://revfitz.com

Cover Design by Kyle Perry https://www.kpapparel.net/

The author greatly appreciates you taking the time to read his work. Please consider leaving a review wherever you bought the book, or telling your friends about it, to help him spread the word.

Thank you for supporting my work.

injecting Gonzo into fiction

For everyone I have met on this strange journey
Your stories are indispensable to my growth

Thank you for the breakfast suggestions,
I am *incredibly* sorry for the existential angst I have inflicted on you all

…But not really

Author's Note:

Existential Terror and Breakfast was originally published as a weekly serial over the course of a year and a half with each "episode" posted on a Wednesday with the story progressing "in real time". Contained in these pages is the "first season" of that serial which took place over a ninety day period.

existential TERROR and breakfast
season one

M.P. Fitzgerald

injecting Gonzo into fiction

Seattle

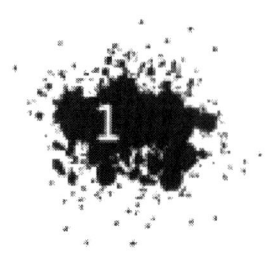

1

Malcolm Steadman is a man who will drown in his own mind. This you should know. You should also know that there is nothing to be done to prevent this. In three months Malcolm will take his first proper plunge. Then he will begin to drown.

There is nothing particularly remarkable about this man, and the specific details of his life are not yet important. He has a job that he does not like, he is very average, and he relishes in fitting in.

You cannot save him.

Malcolm is not especially ambitious, nor is he anymore interesting than your bellybutton. He occasionally drinks in excess and a conversation is something he usually stalls instead of contributing to.

These pages do not concern the life-affirming moments of his life, nor do they contain his exciting adventures. No, these pages concern the moments that Malcolm fails to busy himself, and is thus captured by his own bored mind and rampant existential dread. *No, not dread*, dread is too pedestrian for what he will be gripped by. *Terror*, existential terror. These pages concern his existential terror and breakfast…

…And it begins on a Wednesday.

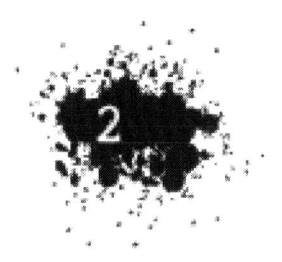

Malcolm Steadman was making toast when a terribly profound, and deeply troubling thought bore its way violently to the forefront of his consciousness. The morning before this was as listless and routine as any Wednesday morning. It was mildly agitating as the minutes had trudged by while his toast was cooking, but otherwise did not have any qualities worth noting or comparing to any other moment. Then the toast popped. The thought came suddenly.

His toast was a little burnt, just enough for him to notice the layer of black carbon that the bread had become. It had just occurred to him just how immensely long it had taken the universe to create carbon, and therefore toast, and he was not prepared for the sheer weight of that concept. Carbon, like most matter, is forged in the raging hot fusion of stars, a process that is so impressively powerful it forces atoms to combine. Not enough can be said about how mighty this force of nature is. It took a full 200 million years after the universe was birthed screaming into the ether for a star to form and for the forging of matter to begin. These stars would burn and burn, crushing atoms into each other to create the furnaces of gods for billions of years. Billions. Only after they died, a process so violent and terrible that their corpses became abominations and eat light, could carbon be released. After a star explodes and turns into physics breaking monsters would carbon scatter into the unfeeling and uncaring void that is space, and eventually congregate into planets. This process, of stars exploding dust and debris would go on for ten and a half billion years before the Earth would finally form. Ten billion years of exchanged energy to create a speck of rock streaming through infinity.

That rock would ferment and stew for another billion years before the most primitive form of life would be formed, and another 2 billion years would pass before life would produce sexually. All this time, the used up energy of stars would pass from one life to another. Carbon would be eaten, and stolen, from life after life, leaving an unbroken chain of dead organisms behind. Humans joined this greedy dance of thievery just 200 thousand years ago. It was not this process that set Malcolm into a panic attack. It is what we did with all this potential energy that freaked him out. Malcolm sat down, his muscles giving in to the burden of gravity. His toast was getting cold.

All of this, all of this potential energy, none of it disappearing but simply passing from star to rock to life endlessly. Shouldn't it amount to something? This, this was the thought that did him in, that truly made his existential terror peak: all of that time and carbon was wasted when we immortalized Honey Boo Boo. She would last longer than the pyramids. Traveling at the speed of light is the broadcast signal of the reality TV show "Here Comes Honey Boo Boo" growing bigger and moving outward as a sphere into space. When the Earth is consumed by fire and eaten by our sun, Honey Boo Boo will remain. When the pyramids of Giza topple, and even the words of the Torah are forgotten, the broadcast signal of Honey Boo Boo will remain. The pinnacle of Reality TV would even outlast the plaque left on the moon by Apollo Astronauts. Our greatest triumph. Honey Boo Boo won't be the only one either. Hitler was the first world leader to be broadcast into space and that broadcast will likely outlast all of the visible stars in the sky. Humanity at its worst, leaking into eternity like a urine stain that will never wash out. The death of numerous stars, the feeding fest of life, all of that carbon, wasted. All of that carbon. Wasted.

The injustice of it was too much.

Malcolm ate his toast.

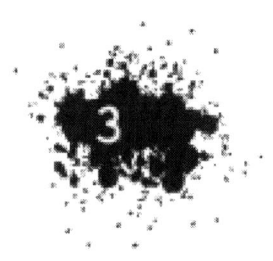

A vague feeling of guilt echoed above Malcolm's unforgiving hangover as light intruded into his eyes. The existential panic attack he would be having soon would be worse. Every bit of movement was like a heavy burden as he marched out of his bed. He was starting to think that waking up was a mistake. The crux of the morning was how he had gotten home. Malcolm indulged to the point that he had blacked out, and consequently had no recollection of how he had gotten home. Strewn across his now sordid house was a full set of clothing that he had worn the night previous and bafflingly enough there was a fully completed jigsaw puzzle on his coffee table.

Malcolm Steadman is not exactly known for his deductive skills, and is certainly no Sherlock Holmes, but it occurred to him that he had walked home from the pub, removed his clothing, and expertly assembled the jigsaw puzzle. He had done that, all without being conscious of doing it. A terrible dread was slowly building around him. This suggested to him that consciousness was not a necessary component to the complexities of his life.

The finished puzzle before him was one that he had owned for a couple of years. He had originally bought it after he had promised himself that he would take up a hobby and be more productive with his life. This puzzle would sit on his bookcase, gathering dust, acting as a testament to his inactive lifestyle. Now, it sat finished, mocking his fragile sense of agency. After he had blacked out, his body acted in an autopilot that was not just set to his basic instinctive needs, but also to his aspirations. If he was capable of deciding to do it without being sentient, was his consciousness, or his ego, actually in control at all? Was his sense of "I" or "me" the pilot to his life, or was it just a constant commentary on the automated actions that he would do with or without it? Was Malcolm in fact, just an awkward automaton with the illusion of free will? He had ceased to notice his menacing headache.

The terrible dread had turned into a full panic attack.

His heart raced and palpitated, his breath was labored, the false sense that he was dying hung in his mind. The puzzle was of course, unaffected by this. Here was the worse part of it: if his sense of being was an unnecessary commentary with the illusion of agency, then his panic attack was doubly so. Him being upset about never having freewill was totally frivolous. That, he thought, was *cruel*. Did it matter that he thought it was cruel? What was the use of his sentient protestations to a life of automation that did not need his permission to automate? If this is how it was going to be (or had always been), wouldn't it be less of a hassle if he was always blacked out? He imagined going about his usual day-to-day life, walking, eating, conversing, and yes, even solving puzzles, all without him being "him".

His panic attack faded out of focus as his hangover fell back into the foreground. This was no better. He was still experiencing unpleasantness even though it appeared that experiencing that unpleasantness was a feature that was not needed. Could it be that the only true difference between him and his puzzle, was that the puzzle did not pretend "to be"? Only one of them insisted that they had volition.

Whether he truly decided to do it, or was preordained to, Malcolm Steadman began to spitefully, and violently, kick the puzzle before him to death. Each vengeful kick only enhanced the intensity of his hangover. He was vaguely aware that he was only spiting himself.

Then he got ready for work.

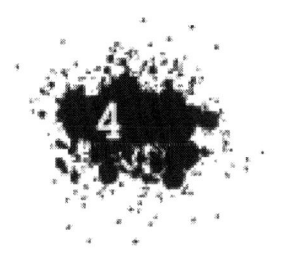

It was a Wednesday morning and Malcolm thought his oatmeal looked bleak. He quickly corrected himself in his mind because he had actually meant "bland". His oatmeal looked bland. It bothered him that bleak still made more sense in his head. That *was* actually what he meant. There was no reason to correct himself. His oatmeal was bleak. Incredibly bleak. He realized now that bleak was the right word because it was bland, but more importantly, because it was a symptom of something else.

It could not be overstated that it was a Wednesday morning. This was important to his current crisis because of the very nature of Wednesday mornings. Malcolm had just realized that he could easily transplant any Wednesday morning in his past with any other and that it would make no difference. All of them were a blur of blandness, routine, and most importantly, impotent acceptance that it was always the same. Sure, he could make promises, and certainly *had* made promises, to do something exciting or change a habit, but ultimately it would not materialize. The Wednesdays that he wasn't working, or fulfilling his dreary mid-week routines were anomalies. If he had committed to going skydiving next week wouldn't the next hundred Wednesdays be filled with the same mundane things they had always had? Even if he had committed to always do something exciting on a Wednesday for the rest of his life, wouldn't these monochrome actions simply migrate themselves to another day of the week? Wednesday mornings were a truer representation of his life than the exciting things he had done and bragged to his coworkers about. The oatmeal was bleak because it was symbolic of his very nature. Malcolm Steadman was a dry, flaky, and bland individual. Just like his oatmeal.

He wondered why it had gotten so bad. There was no warning ahead of time, his life had just gradually stayed the same. There was no one to tell him that routine and habit would pile up to eat away at his time and leave a collage of memories that were indistinct from each other. Was there something numbing about this, was nobody able to yell danger because it came with an impotent acceptance?

His oatmeal was overcooked.

Malcolm took a moment to desperately remedy the situation, knowing ahead of time that it would be in vain. He rummaged through his cabinet, trying not to think about how long his spices had sat there. After manically pushing things aside he found his target: hot sauce. In one movement he had jumped from his cabinet and was already drowning his oatmeal in a viscous red liquid. He knew that this would be one of those Wednesdays that would be lost and relentlessly buried in a mountain of cloned Wednesdays, but he could not bear the thought of letting this one be the same. After shoveling his spoon into his breakfast...no...his *statement*, Malcolm brought the food to his mouth and immediately regretted doing so. The regret was not from the searing meat that was now his tongue, but because it was really just a token victory. He realized now that it was not the sea of bland Wednesdays behind him that bothered him; it was the grand ocean ahead of him that he would have to endure.

The mundanities of life had to be opiates. They were numbing so that they would go unnoticed. The real villain here was time. Life, in its moment to moment beats, is unbearable. It is as boring as it is long, and it is *very* long. Now that Malcolm was fully aware of the nature of Wednesdays he was immune to its opiatic effects meant to shield him from the terrible existential horribleness to come. He would now notice, and have to push through, every bleak Wednesday that he would have to experience in real-time.

Malcolm did not eat the rest of his oatmeal because it was too spicy. He did not eat it because it was far too bleak.

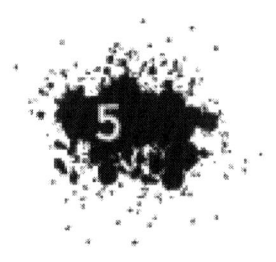

Malcolm Steadman had been staring at his toaster waiting for his pop-tart to finish cooking for what seemed like a full ten minutes. That is because it *had* been a full ten minutes. It took Malcolm another two minutes to realize this. This upset him.

The toaster *had* to be broken.

This, in any normal circumstances would be less of a problem, but Malcolm had been experiencing a string of terrible epiphanies too profound for him to handle and earnestly just needed a break from such heavy thinking. He was just supposed to eat his toast, ignore the injustices of carbon, pretend that he had agency and go to work, and ignore the bleak ocean of banalities and Wednesdays ahead of him. The toaster breaking, however, meant that he was now thinking about entropy.

Entropy.

Everything, no matter how grand and majestic, or small and useless, ends. If there is one constant, one rule that everything must adhere to, it is that everything is a slave to entropy. Malcolm, of course, is no exception. He realized that he had owned the toaster for nearly ten years. When it was gifted to him he was a much younger man, one with endless hope and a sense that everything in his life would work out. Yet each day since he had popped his first slice of bread into the toaster, the appliance, as well as himself, saw an almost microscopic bit of wear and tear. It *slightly* horrified him to know now that each act of toasting bread had actually harmed the toaster little by little until the filament in it had burned out. It *severely* horrified himself to know how much he had changed in that time.

The endless hope, the sense that everything would work out, had dwindled. He was jaded now, jaded and tired. He was ten years older and still working for very little. Things had not worked out. Things had not worked out, and he was just getting older. Slowly. The minuscule changes in his body and life would continue to happen, and without his permission, until he was no more. Malcolm would someday be as dead as the toaster. On top of that, he would be there to see it all happen, at a snail's pace through time. The worst of it was that he would be aware that he was aging, that Death's visit was only inching closer and there would be no one to save him. He would get older, weaker, and he would lose his faculties. His mind would slip from him and he would forget everything, and with enough time, everything would forget about him.

The universe would go on without him of course, but even that was not eternal. Decay had been happening to it the moment the big bang exploded it into the ether. There was not a single thing in the universe that could fight entropy because the universe itself lost before the fight had begun. Just like Malcolm himself, the universe would lose its luster. It would slowly grow weaker as stars exploded and grew further apart. Everything would break. Time and entropy would eat them all until even they themselves would cease to exist. A horrifying monster deaf and blind to its action, a monster so fierce that it would devour everything without prejudice, and it would do it slow. Painfully, horrifically slow. This monster, Malcolm entertained, had all of the patience because it knew it was destined to win.

Though it should seem obvious, it dawned on him now that what bothered him about this was that there was no protecting the things that made life so precious. The counted and recorded knowledge of generations and generations of people. Music that had sparked great emotions and inspired one to forget how to be embarrassed and dance. The breathless silence of a couple as they kiss for the first time as spouses in a wedding photo. Entropy would destroy them, and entropy would destroy them with as much thought as it gave even the worse things about existence: *none*. All would be forgotten at the heat death of the universe.

Malcolm ate his uncooked pop-tart from the toaster...

He would only find out later when he came home from work that the toaster was just simply unplugged.

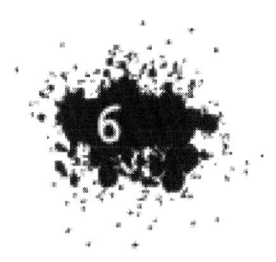

He was just trying to find something whimsical. Honestly. Malcolm had no intention of triggering another philosophical anxiety attack. The existential terror he had been experiencing every week was wearing on him. For the record, he let most of these moments pass and did not give it another thought until another one would occur. It was his subconscious, however, that was suffering. He was depressed now and lacked the energy to do the things that he had loved. He was not yet fully conscious of what was causing it, at least, not yet.

He was really just trying to find something whimsical. Something that would lighten his mood and his day. As Malcolm Steadman sipped on his black, morning coffee he landed on a web-page about apes learning sign language. Apes and sign language! There could not be anything more pleasant and whimsical! Malcolm caught himself making an involuntary high pitched noise in glee as he clicked on the article. This, *this* was the distraction he needed this morning. He was wrong.

He read about Washoe's abduction. He read about Koko's dead kittens. He let out an involuntary yell of terror.

There was a pattern that emerged between Washoe the chimpanzee and Koko the gorilla, a pattern of pain and possible self-awareness. Washoe was captured in West Africa by the United States Air Force to be used as testing for the space program in the 1960's, but she ended up being taught sign language at the University of Reno Nevada. There she learned 350 signs, including "cry". Koko the gorilla, however, was born in the San Francisco Zoo before she was loaned to Dr. Patterson who famously taught her how to sign. She was able to learn more than a thousand different signs, including "cry". The bitterness Malcolm now tasted, was not from his coffee, but from an epiphany: Was misery a side effect of language? If so, did we spread it unintentionally to the apes?

If one is not able to describe the trauma that they felt, if one did not have a word for it, was it real? Was misery only a condition of sentient thought because it had a definition? Before these female apes were taught words like "cry" or "bad", did they live in a blissful ignorance? What was the purpose of communicating these things to them?

Chimpanzees and gorillas don't naturally cry. They shed no tears. It is not a natural concept for them. But Koko and Washoe "cried" when informed of tragedies.

Washoe, a previously happy and healthy chimpanzee who was possibly not self-aware beforehand was taught the magic of language, and for what purpose? To be miserable? Malcolm read that the first time she signed "cry" one of her handlers had told Washoe that she was absent for many weeks because her child had died. Koko signed "cry" when she was told that her pet kitten died, and again when her friend, Robin Williams committed suicide. **Koko saw neither of these things happen!** It was not as if Robbin Williams visited her often, did she need to know he was dead?

These scientists gifted these apes with language, they taught them the biggest cognitive breakthrough for intelligent species and with it gave them self-awareness. Reportedly, Washoe went through "an identity crisis" when she met other chimpanzees because "she believed she was human". These scientist illuminated these ape's minds and then dumped all of their garbage and sadness into them. With this gift of knowledge came concepts like "sad", and now these apes were *terribly* aware of it.

Malcolm was not aware that he had spilled his coffee on his keyboard. He would only notice it after he found that his mouth was agape for ten whole minutes and was now sore.

He was not aware of his pain until he thought of the word "sore".

If the "ineffable" was only brought into reality after language could describe it, were the apes better off without it? Koko had known the pain of losing someone dear to her because she now knew what that meant, and no one thought about just lying to her.

Was Malcolm better off without knowledge or language? Would he have given consent to learning it if he had known what burdens it would bare?

Malcolm cleaned his keyboard and pretended that he did not see the symbolism of the tool. He resigned himself not to seek out whimsy for the rest of the week. He did not make more coffee, and he was becoming increasingly misanthropic.

7

To say that Malcolm Steadman was currently doing nothing would be erroneous. Yes, in the normal sense of the nomenclature Malcolm was doing "nothing", but in fact Malcolm was always doing something. At the moment he was sitting, he was staring into space and he was letting his breakfast cereal get soggy. Malcolm was breathing, and each breath he took burned a minuscule amount of calories and replenished his body with precious oxygen. If you asked Malcolm what he did with his morning he might look embarrassed, and as he would avoid your eye contact he would shuffle his feet and moan the word "nothing", but again, this was far from the truth.

Malcolm was not proud of his life, he considered it a vague failure and had a constant nagging feeling that if he did not do anything with it he would suddenly find that it was too late to start. He was constantly comparing his life to others. What they had and he didn't, whether it was a healthy and loving relationship with others, or more money and a better career, seemed to justify his notion that he had done nothing with his life. This did not motivate him to change it, though he might swear in the moment that he would, but it did make him sad. Malcolm was often sad. If he had taken the time to be less harsh on himself, and had considered just how miraculous his life was, maybe he would be less sad. But he won't. He would continue his habits and things *will* get *worse. So much worse.*

The miracle that was Malcolm Steadman was impossibly more wondrous than he would ever give himself credit for. As he sat and did "nothing" **86 billion neurons** in his brain worked together to create thought and consciousness. Malcolm's mind was a series of an immense number of cells working together to create the world's most awesome natural computer. Even as he listlessly looked down at his soggy breakfast, doing "nothing" these 86 billion neurons were working on his subconscious level to work out a math problem he had merely glanced at earlier and had "forgotten" about. As he shifted his weight to be more comfortable in his chair, and continue to feel bad about himself, this network of neurons passed on information from his senses to perceive the incredibly complex reality in front of him and it would render this perception faster than any rocket could travel. Malcolm Steadman was a miracle, and he hated himself.

Yes, Malcolm would never be able to perceive the universe around him *correctly*. There would never be a single thing he would think about the universe that would be correct. Yes, Malcolm would never be able to perceive the universe correctly, **but he could perceive it**. That, in itself, was the greatest testament to Malcolm Steadman being great. The universe, as vast and confusing and random and chaotic and grand that it was could be *looked* upon. It could be judged and thought about and that was incredible. If Malcolm would take just a second to consider this, the trivialities of his worries could vanish. He won't though.

He felt as soggy and limp as his breakfast.

Of course, Malcolm had a right to feel this way. He had the right to feel any way he wanted. It's just a shame that he did. At his age, Malcolm Steadman had now lived longer than the majority of his ancestors. The bulk of them lived in fear and mostly just aspired to procreate and to be safe. Malcolm had the luxury to let his food slowly spoil in front of him in the comfort of his warm home and not have to worry when he would eat next. The fact that so many of his ancestors had survived long enough to produce young, and eventually him was staggering. Malcolm had the time to consider the universe around him, he had time to weigh complex mysteries and philosophize about them. In actuality, Malcolm was an incredibly lucky and blessed individual whose existence was impossibly miraculous! ...and he felt depressed.

Malcolm was always doing something, and each and every moment he existed was immensely wondrous. Yet he perceived that he was doing nothing. He would continue to compare his life to others who were equally as wondrous, and he would feel bad about himself. He would never realize how divine he was. At this moment, Malcolm would miss an epiphany that was affirming and important: that he was, and always had been impressive. Instead, Malcolm would toss his unfinished cereal and march his way to a job that he hated. Instead, Malcolm would feel ashamed for being a waste.

Malcolm Steadman will dial the suicide hotline in 90 days.

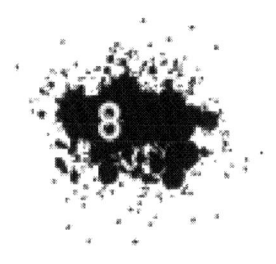

Malcolm Steadman will dial the suicide hotline in 83 days.

The sweet smell of citrus coming from the half-peeled grapefruit was a stark contrast to Malcolm's sour mood. In an uncharacteristic moment of resolve, Malcolm Steadman had decided that he was going to start to eat healthy foods. This would last a full three days before Malcolm would consume two whole McDonald's breakfast sandwiches in one morning. He would not switch back to grapefruit for another month. This current resolve (yet untouched by McDonald's) however had manifested in other aspects of his life. As he slowly peeled the large fruit Malcolm passively took part in an online application process for a new job.

Malcolm hated his job. He needed a change of pace and after drunkenly ranting to his peers about his terrible job the night before had decided to do something about it. The application he had in front of him had gone beyond the point of simple work information and was now asking him to rate different statements on how much he agreed with them on a sliding scale. None of these were difficult and Malcolm casually answered "somewhat agree" to the majority of them as he continued to peel his giant fruit. Then he came to question "No. 9". His grapefruit and his mood now had the quality "bitter" in common. This was the question:

No. 9: I am happy with my life.

Please choose one:

Strongly agree. Somewhat agree. Neither agree or disagree. Disagree. Strongly disagree.

Malcolm was **not** happy with his life. Malcolm was often very sad and hated many aspects of his day-to-day routines. This was NOT a fair question. Of course he was not happy, why else would he be looking for a better job?! Why did this matter to this company's HR department? If he answered honestly would he not be interviewed for the job? *This*, Malcolm thought, *is bullshit*. If the application were made of paper, and he was honest, he would circle "Strongly disagree" heavily so that the pen left deep track marks into it. He would not even have that simple satisfaction as the application was online. He hated his life, and now he was robbed of that symbolic gesture of spite by a faceless HR web developer.

What did his happiness have to do with being qualified to work? He knew ahead of time that it was very likely that there was an algorithm behind the application that would decide if his application even had the chance to be seen by human eyes. It was very possible that it was this question that would decide that.

Malcolm was no longer peeling his fruit. He was unconsciously stabbing it with his fork.

Happiness, he thought, *was being quantified as a value of worth*. A state of being that relied on a number of brain chemicals and a certain disposition was now the obstacle Malcolm had to face so that he could try to obtain that exact state. Malcolm was long aware that his culture had placed "the pursuit of happiness" into the forefront of the zeitgeist, what he was not prepared for was that it was now a necessity for living in that culture. Malcolm was not happy. Was Malcolm worthless?

Of course, Malcolm could simply lie and choose one of the "agree" statements, but what was the appropriate amount of happiness? If he chose "strongly agree" would they write him off as an eccentric? Further, Malcolm *did not want to lie* on the application. He took great pride in his qualifications and his references and never felt the need to lie for a job before. What if after reading his response they called one of his references who knew damn well that Malcolm had a *terrible* disposition? Would they lie for him?

He realized now that it was not the question that bothered him, but that it was the overall expectation society had placed on him to be happy. There was no such thing as permanent happiness. Malcolm was happy sometimes. No one was truly always happy. Yet society pretended that this was the norm. Whole philosophies and religions were written for the attainment of happiness. From Aristotle's vice and virtues and the pursuit of "eudaimonia" to the Bible's "Kingdom of Heaven", lasting happiness was hotly debated. Malcolm had spent much time reading about different paths and promises he could take to be happy from great thinkers, prophets, and even charlatans and quacks. Being happy with your life was the greatest problem humankind had ever faced, and here was a questionnaire for a menial job that could deny that possibility to him if he already had not obtained it!

Malcolm lied. He circled "somewhat agree". Then he

ate his giant fruit. He felt embarrassed later that day that something so small had set him off. His next existential crisis would be worse.

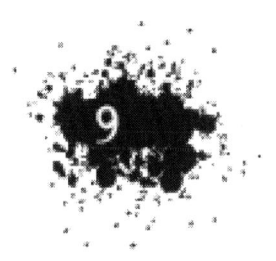

*Author's note: Due to the very boring nature of the details of other people's dreams, the specific details of Malcolm Steadman's dream has been **redacted** to keep the reader from losing interest.*

Malcolm Steadman will dial the suicide hotline in 76 days.

A wisp of steam rose steadily from Malcolm's Coffee as he slowly adjusted to his day. Sleep had mostly escaped him the night before, and what little he was able to catch tormented him. That was not hyperbole. Malcolm was fully aware of the irony that the sleep he desperately needed he didn't want, at least not until he had started dreaming. His dream, *dear lord his dream*. Malcolm shuddered at the thought of it and accidentally spilled some coffee on the front of his boxers. The burning sensation was preferable to the horrors of his dream. In a moment, Malcolm would lament that his dream paled to the realities of his coming epiphany.

The thing Malcolm couldn't shake as he slowly sipped his coffee was just how real his dream felt. When he dreamt that he was holding a ▇▇▇▇▇ and carried it to the ▇▇▇▇▇▇▇▇▇▇▇ orifice, was it not as real feeling to him now as his coffee had felt that had just burned him? Sure, Malcolm Steadman knew that he was awake currently, but he was equally confident of that fact during his anxiety dream. His dream than was just an extremely convincing lie that he had fallen for. Now that he was awake the absurdities of him bounding over an ▮▮▮▮▮ so that he could ▮ ▮▮▮▮▮ and sup milk from the wombs of terror and ▮▮▮▮▮▮▮▮▮ were obviously the materials of a very disturbing dream and had no place in the reality that he now resided in, but he was absolutely spell-bound and convinced of them as they occurred. Could he be a fool to that same spell now only to find himself waking for a second time? No, Malcolm was convinced that he was awake, but that was not the problem.

His senses, the tools that he relied on to inform him of his environment, had lied to him. His sight in the dream informed him of the ▮▮▮▮ cupcakes that were not real, his tactile senses made said ▮▮▮ cupcakes feel like ice, and even his taste had colluded in the deceit and made him think they tasted like ▮▮▮▮▮▮▮▮ your mother. Each one of these senses he depended on to get through the day and he had trusted them completely and now he had just learned that they were liars! He was not foolish enough to trust someone who had lied to him even once, did this mean that his senses were not to be trusted?

Malcolm's coffee was getting cold.

He was incensed now. Malcolm felt truly betrayed, he could not think of anything more intimate to him than his senses, and they were deceitful liars. He decided to go over his dream fully and recounted that in it he was ...▮▮▮▮▮ ▮ ▮ ▮▮▮▮▮▮▮▮▮▮▮▮ the demi-moon ▮▮▮▮? And that he

was attached to his father by an umbilical cord. It was pretty obvious as to what Freud would say about that.

A growing panic had gripped him now. If Malcolm could not trust his senses, then he could not trust anything they told him about the external world and therefore the external world could be a lie. His now lukewarm black coffee may not exist. There was now nothing in Malcolm's life that he could trust to be real. There was no memory, no matter how fond to him or vivid in detail that he could trust to be real either. Without a basic trust in the information that his senses gave him, everything around him fell apart into an existential insecurity.

Malcolm had forgotten to breathe for an entire minute.

If he could not trust his senses all of reality as he had understood it could be false. If that reality was in fact just a false manifestation in his mind than Malcolm Steadman was alone. Truly and horrifically alone. If the external world did not exist, than the people who populated it did not either. Malcolm's entire life experience and the people that he had held dear could easily be a cruel joke. What logical ground did he have to stand on to argue for an external world? A deep wave of sadness had washed over Malcolm now, cleansing him only of his most basic of confidence. Not only could the world around him be a retched construct, but it was one that he had *no control over*. He could be the only thinking thing in existence, and he was not even the god of his own reality. These falsities would play out in front of him regardless of his consent, and no amount of effort would make him less alone. Reality could be a monstrous vignette playing in front of him independent of his wishes. Lies. All of it lies.

All of this because Malcolm had dreamt he was ███████. God damn Descartes.

Malcolm drank his cold coffee and did the dishes. He still went to work that day, or at least he believed he did.

Malcolm Steadman will dial the suicide hotline in 69 days.

Right now, Malcolm Steadman is shaving. He will cut himself later, so there is that to look forward to. This is not the time or place where he will have an existential crisis. Malcolm will not deal with the ineffable struggles of being conscious nor will he experience a debilitating sense of ominous dread that will stick with him for the rest of the day...Well, at least not yet. This panic attack will happen later, while he interviews for a job.

Malcolm was currently shaving for that job interview. He had scheduled the interview during a morning that he was supposed to work at his current job and was confident enough at that time about his prospects for being hired that he just did not show up to work and did not call in about it. This was not something that he had done before, but this was the *new* Malcolm, *this* Malcolm was taking charge and would change his life for the better! Of course, he will not get the job because of his aforementioned panic attack, and because in reality there was no "new" Malcolm. Malcolm dipped his disposable razor into his sink to wet it and began to shave.

"New" Malcolm was confident and started to whistle

merrily as he slowly stroked his razor down his cheek. He was upbeat this Morning and for once in his anxious life enjoyed a tinge of anticipation. *This*, he thought, *was going to be a good day*. What Malcolm did not know yet was that he will bump into his manager from his current job in the lobby of the building that he will interview in. That meeting will be step one towards his avalanche of dread. It will actually get better after that before it gets exponentially worse.

What will shock him when he meets his manager is that she will be equally shocked and embarrassed to see him as well. As it will turn out, she was not happy with her job either and applied for the same job as Malcolm to change her life. What will shock Malcolm even more, is that the conversation he will have with her will be perfectly pleasant. Malcolm did not think of his manager as a pleasant person, and had actually wanted to quit his job in part because he thoroughly disliked her. The conversation that they will have will start with an air of awkwardness as they both realize that neither of them showed up for work, and that only one of them will get the job. This will pass quickly though as they will talk as equals for the first time. It will be surprising to both of them to find out that they have so much in common and time will seem to pass quickly before Malcolm will be called in for the interview first. They will both wish that the conversation lasted longer. On his way to being interviewed a terrible realization will seize him.

"New" and "empowered" Malcolm was no longer paying attention to his shaving and instead was focusing more on whistling. He pressed his razor roughly against his skin... But he was fine. He won't be when he freezes midway through his stride to the interviewer and realize what an unfeeling monster he had been to his manager. He will find out through their conversation that she hated her job because she was a manager and that it forced her to act cold towards her subordinates. She was constantly hounded by her higher-ups for results that were not possible and when her bosses made a mistake they would put the blame on her. She was miserable and she despised herself. Malcolm had never considered that his manager was a vulnerable person. She was always just a source of stress for him. Here was a perfectly pleasant woman who Malcolm had dehumanized and disliked for such trivial reasons because she was his manager.

The razor was not being held tightly during Malcolm's second run at his face and would slip... out of his hand. He was fine.

Both of their jobs could have been better if Malcolm had just reached out to a clearly stressed individual and conversed with her casually. Where was his empathy during that time? Could Malcolm's sense of empathy be so easily turned off because of a preconceived social role that was entirely constructed by his job? Was the line between him being an empathetic and caring person, and him being unfeeling and cold so thin? If it was that thin, how close was unfeeling and cold from being a psychopath? Malcolm will recall how often he took part in schadenfreude every time he saw his manager fail. He would muse delightfully with his peers and celebrate every failure behind her back. None of this seemed cruel or antagonistic at the time, it would be a fun part of his day and Malcolm would often look forward to it. He will resolve that these feelings were sociopathic in nature because of the general lack of empathy. *Anyone who looks forward to someone's misfortune and pain*, Malcolm will think, *is a monster*.

His razor cut him just behind his jaw. Pain! A sharp

and demanding pain grabbed his attention now as blood dripped off of him and became diluted in the sink's water.

Malcolm stopped whistling.

When Malcolm leaves his apartment and walks to the bus stop to carry him to his appointment, while he waits tentatively for the bus to arrive, he won't think of the other passengers in front of him as people and will be annoyed at how slow they were getting on. When he finds himself a seat he won't think of the old man beside him as a grandfather who can't afford his pain medication. He will see him as an obstruction in the seat that he wanted, and he will touch the band-aid on his neck and focus on his own pain. When he bombs his interview because he is too busy feeling guilty about how he treated his manager behind her back and arrives back on the bus, he will see things differently. He will not be annoyed. The "inconvenience" of the schizophrenic homeless man beside him? He will see how lonely and tragic that human's life is. The "incompetent obstruction" ahead of him having trouble paying its fare? A woman and a mother.

But he hasn't left his apartment yet, he has not learned those lessons. Malcolm finished shaving and, despite his wound, admired his work and smiled. There was a full day ahead of him and he was excited about his prospects. He left his bathroom with pep in his step and laughed to himself as he imagined the look on his manager's face as she found out he was not coming to work.

He imagined it wrong.

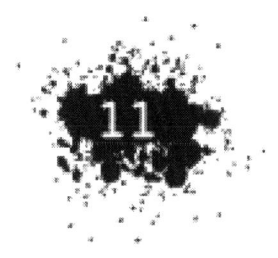

Malcolm Steadman will dial the suicide hotline in 62 days.

Malcolm Steadman was ignoring the aggressively symbolic nature of the plain bagel he had just bought as a mirror to his personality with an abrasive sort of misanthropy that he and only the British had perfected. As he had no hands free, Malcolm desperately tried to ignore the default ringtone on his phone and how that reflected on his lack of creativity as he trekked home. He started to whistle then in a fatal attempt to both drown the electronic buzzing out and to counter the rising self-loathing that was feeding off of his inadequacies. Mr. Steadman did not get the job he had interviewed for. This blow to his self-esteem was entirely his own fault. He was unprepared to deal with the fact that the constant existential terror that he felt might suggest that he was going mad. Now unemployed, Malcolm carried a plain bagel with cream cheese and a black coffee home to keep some semblance of routine now that his main responsibility was gone. That is when he saw it: sitting in a shop's display was a plastic dinosaur that was brightly colored. It filled him with a powerful nostalgia for his childhood. He believed strongly that whimsy would brighten his day and bought the toy. He had not learned his lesson on his whimsical self-prescriptions, apparently.

Once he was settled home, and had begun to devour his cheap breakfast, Malcolm began to turn the toy dinosaur in his hand and contemplate it affectionately. He had owned this same type of toy as a boy and fondly remembered playing with it and the joy that it had brought him. The aforementioned existential terror that was possibly driving Malcolm to madness? It was coming. The bane of Malcolm's existence now was that without a job he was running out of ways to distract himself with the gained time he had in his day. When Malcolm isn't distracted he begins to contemplate the things around him, and as we have previously seen this typically results in a philosophical disaster for him. He figured that this toy would be a slight reprieve from this. Oh, how he was wrong.

Even alone Malcolm was too self-conscious to actually play with the dinosaur, though that might be the *exact* sort of distraction he needed. Instead, Malcolm noticed through his close observation of the toy a slight seam where some plastic had seeped out during the molding process and had hardened. His nostalgic sense of wonder was wearing thin. Malcolm knew that plastic was forged from crude oil. Malcolm's "flight or fight" sense was triggered suddenly as the expansive length of time for this toy to have taken form attacked his delicate psyche.

Malcolm had failed to distract himself.

Crude oil is the culmination of dead plants and animals spread across the millennia. An uncounted amount of life, with all of its fallacies and wondrous miracles, would be born, live, and die to create just a small amount of this organic deluge. From the time humankind had first stood upright, to the moment that a select few got to tour the moon was but a fraction of the time it had taken for the amount of oil that was necessary to make this toy to culminate underground. Whole species would mutate off to create a new branch of evolution and go extinct, leaving behind the sludge that ultimately became this colorful plaything. Oil, at its most basic level, is a graveyard for the mass amount of failed life and potential that graced the earth for only a whisper in time...and Malcolm had *played* with this graveyard.

In a panic, Malcolm dropped the toy and began breathing heavily. *He was not going to do this again*. He was not going to go down this path to frightening epiphanies. He simply did not have the constitution for it. The fact that his moods and that his sanity had become so frail and that they were so suggestible to these panic attacks made him feel incredibly impotent. When had the slightest of events or the smallest of objects become such a powerful catalyst to set him off? When had things become so overblown? If he had explained these episodes to someone else would they understand, or would the minuscule nature of these catalysts make him seem crazy?

Of course, Malcolm was going to think about the toy, he was **ABSOLUTELY** going to follow the winding path to a frightening epiphany.

It was in his most basic nature.

The toy that was now on the floor was a perverse monument to the massive amount of time and life it contained in its form. The crude oil it was made up of, through the wonders of chemistry was morphed into an inaccurate visage of the life it was made up of. This dinosaur toy that Malcolm had bought to cheer him up through misguided nostalgia was made up of dead dinosaurs. Here on his floor sat a false idol to the dead and through humankind's modern alchemy took the form of a creature that merely resembled the complex animals it once was in only the most basic sense. The punchline? It would likely stay in this form longer than humankind would be around. The earth would be littered with these plastic monuments long after humans were forgotten and their temples ruined.

Someday, Malcolm's remains would add to the pools of crude oil, and maybe it too would be turned into a plastic toy.

Malcolm could not bring himself to throw the toy away, and not just because it had cost him money. Though this toy dinosaur had become the bane of his morning, and although it had added to the weight of his anxieties, he kept it. Throwing it away just seemed like such a waste considering the origin of its chemicals. Malcolm calmed himself down and finished his breakfast and considered seeing a psychoanalyst.

During his existential terror Malcolm failed to notice that when his phone had buzzed earlier, a company had called him to set up an interview. They will not call back and he will not get a second chance.

When he was done with his coffee he threw the plastic cap away.

12

The prospect that Malcolm was going mad was one that he now had to give some urgent attention to. When his existential panic attacks were merely affecting his mood or causing him to spill his coffee, they were benign inconveniences. He had first waved these attacks off as being normal side-effects of stress, the past couple of weeks, however, they had caused him to miss not one, but two whole opportunities for a job. These panic attacks had now just directly affected his livelihood. He needed someone to talk to about it. He needed to know if other people experienced the occasional existential terror like he had, he needed to know that he was not alone in this. If he was...

Malcolm Steadman's current problem was that he had nobody to talk to. He could not talk to any of his friends about his problem because all of his adult friends were actually friendly coworkers, and now that he no longer had a job he lacked immediate access to them. Of course, if he could talk to them their advice might end up being polite and friendly which Malcolm figured, was the worst possible advice one could get. He needed the advice of someone paid to talk to him. Ideally, he would talk to a therapist of some kind but now that he had no job he could not immediately afford to pay for one. An idea had struck him just then, but the nature of it troubled him as being more proof that he was going mad. Who else could he talk to that was being paid to listen to him? *Customer service.*

He would find the number to his internet provider's customer service line under the pretense that his service was not working, and then spring his problems on an impartial operator that was paid not to hang up on him. It was either an unconventional, but brilliant idea, or it was a sign that he was going utterly and completely bat-shit-insane. After pondering it for a moment he decided that the customer service representative could weigh in on it at the end of the call and dialed the number.

The customer service representative introduced herself over the phone as "Michelle" and asked what "technical difficulty" Malcolm was experiencing in a monotone that was almost sonorous in its deadness. Malcolm lied to Michelle and told her that his internet router's blue light was flashing and that his internet was slow knowing that his router had no such light of that color, this forced Michelle to refer to some technical notes to try and find the meaning of such a problem, it was during this lull in their conversation that Malcolm took action. "Do you ever feel terrible existential dread?" Malcolm asked. He meant for the question to sound casual and intended to tone it as simple small talk, but the brief pause on the other end signaled that he had utterly failed at it. "What?" Michelle responded. Malcolm knew that he had a chance to come back from the awkwardness and tried: "Do you ever panic because of an epiphany or, er, something?"

He failed.

"Like what?" Michelle asked. Malcolm Started from the beginning. Did she ever think about the injustice of carbon, that there was so much potential energy behind it and that we had wasted it in making toy dinosaurs or by broadcasting *Honey Boo Boo*? Had she ever doubted her own free will after a night of drinking? Did Wednesdays ever seem to be terribly and irrevocably bleak in how routine they were? Michelle listened patiently, Malcolm ranted on. Do pop-tarts ever make her think about entropy? Does learning the concept of being sad make you sad? Did she ever feel like she was not in control of her life because of a questionnaire? **Had she ever *really* thought about the injustice of carbon?!!** Was the phrase "injustice of carbon" sane sounding? He explained all of these concepts to her in great detail and desperate exasperation. When he was finally out of breath and feeling more vulnerable than ever, he was met with a silence that felt deafening to him.

"Sometimes," Michelle responded.

Michelle was simply trying to be polite and sound sympathetic because Malcolm was a customer, Malcolm mistook this for being genuine. Michelle was actually very bored and had only heard a portion of what he had said. This was *not* the most interesting call she had that day.

Malcolm was relieved. No, he was *vindicated*! His grave (and totally overblown) philosophical panic attacks were now normalized. The weight of him losing his sanity had been lifted and Malcolm felt elated. He was not the only person who felt utterly hopeless and impotent on a weekly basis because he failed to busy himself and notice just how vast and incomprehensible the world was around him. Malcolm felt normal.

"There isn't supposed to be a flashing blue light on that unit sir," Michelle said perplexed.

"Oh look, it is working now, thank you!" Malcolm

replied and hung up the phone.

Malcolm made himself some toast and no longer felt abnormal or odd that the burnt layer on top outraged and incensed him. He smiled as he finished it and thought that everything will be okay.

Everything, he thought again, *will be okay*.

Malcolm will dial the suicide hotline in 55 days.

13. Perceptions Part 1.

The sharply dressed man beside the boy was making him nervous. The boy had taken the city bus countless of times, he was no stranger to the body language of weirdos, and right now, the man beside him was broadcasting a *very* weird body language. For whatever reason, the boy observed, social contracts were broken all of the time at the bus stop. What permission did the weird see in the bus stop that they could break social norms and ignore all social cues? The boy felt an unopened granola bar that his mother had given him for breakfast inside of his pocket and played with it nervously. He was about to open it and eat the pressed dry meal but when he had eyed the sharply dressed man next to him, he decided to hold off on it. The man beside him was staring directly at him now. *God dammit*, the boy thought, *here we go*...

The boy pulled out some earbuds from his backpack and placed one into each of his ears. He quickly found his music app on his phone and played the first thing that popped up on full blast and begun to relax. This was really his best defense for an awkward or unwanted interaction he had from the weirdos. Only the schizophrenic or the most aggressive creeps would not pick up on this social cue. Earbuds were a passive, but universal way of letting everyone around know that the person wearing them DID NOT WANT TO BE BOTHERED. The man was still staring. The boy knew better than to look back, eye contact was always an invitation to these weirdos. It seemed as if the man was closer now, the boy closed his eyes and took a deep breath. Wherever the bus was, it needed to be here right now.

There was a tap on the boy's shoulder now, and his mind went reeling. *What about me wearing earbuds screamed "touch me" to this creep?* he wondered. A short panic ran through his mind as he considered pretending that he did not notice the tap, but his line of thinking was quickly interrupted when the man tapped his shoulder **again**. "Eh, er... excuse me" the sharply dressed man sputtered over the throbbing beats of the boy's music. The fact that the man looked as uncomfortable about the situation as the boy did little to ease the boy's dread as he pulled out the earbud nearest to the man. "Do you know what time it is?" the man asked timidly.

This was suspicious. The man was well dressed. Had he been older, maybe another generation or two this question would not have raised any red flags for the boy, but the man was middle-aged, and he was well dressed. There was no way that this man did not have a smartphone on him, he could easily check that to tell the time. This meant only one thing: the question was an opener, a ruse to get the boy's full attention. This man had ulterior motives. The boy looked down at his own phone and immediately pulled the phone's dial pad up, just in case he had to dial the authorities. "It's seven-thirty" the boy answered, not looking directly at the man. The boy sighed as it seemed that their business was done and put his earbud back on. The man beside him said something that the boy could not make out through his music as the boy gazed onto his dial pad, hoping he didn't have to use it... and then: nothing. The man beside him took a step back.

The boy took a deep breath and sighed with relief. Then the man took a few steps closer.

The well-dressed man was now VERY close to the boy. His shoulders were squared directly at the boy's side and he was looking straight at the boy. He did not touch the boy this time, but it seemed almost dangerous to the boy to try to ignore him now. The boy reached into his pocket and started nervously feeling his granola bar. He then turned slowly and removed both of his earbuds this time and saw that the man looked almost frightened and stepped back, as if he was pushed away by the boy's gaze. A silence fell between the two as if it were a physical divide, one that they each welcomed and feared to remove. It was only then that the boy realized that, like a spider, this weirdo creep was more afraid of him than he of the man.

"Are—" The man started "are you listening to Pink Floyd?" He finally managed. The boy looked back at him with suspicion and answered a simple and curt "yes". He wasn't.

"That line, 'the sun is the same in a relative way but you're older'? Er, uh no, I meant the line 'ten years have got behind you, no one told you when to run, you missed the starting gun'? That one, the one that goes like that, well... It's true" the man babbled at the boy.

The fear between them had waned, but it was only replaced with an awkwardness that was burdensome.

The man continued and stuttered out "I-I was your age when I first heard that line, it was an old song even when I was young, do you understand? I was your age and now... now I'm going in for an interview for a job that is meaningless and I see no way out of it. Every day I realize that more and more that my life has no meaning and I don't know what to do with myself! And what's more, do you know the irony of it?" The boy shook his head in response.

"The irony is that someone DID tell me when to run, someone warned me about not hearing 'the starting gun' and it was that song. Pink Floyd had warned me all of those years ago and I ignored it!" There was a sense of desperation in his voice now "I must've heard that song hundreds of times since and it never lit a fire under my ass to change anything. Don't. Be. Me. Don't grow up to be me. I wish someone told me that, but I'm telling you, I'm telling you now, *this is the starting gun.*"

The bus had finally arrived.

"Do something with your life" the man pleaded.

"Cool," said the boy.

The boy let the man get on the bus first. The man sat up front, the boy went to the very back. Neither of them looked at each other the entire ride.

The boy ate his granola bar.

14
Perceptions Part 2

Malcolm Steadman will dial the suicide hotline in 48 days.

The shady looking boy that stood next to Malcolm Steadman was making him nervous. To be fair, Malcolm was nearly always nervous and had once been set into a philosophical frenzy because of burnt toast, but the boy next to him looked dangerous. Malcolm had taken the city bus enough times to know when he shouldn't turn his back on someone, and right now, everything about this boy told Malcolm that this was definitely one of those times. It did not help that the teenager Malcolm was worrying about had just reached into his pocket to feel something. A knife? Wherever the bus was, it needed to be here right now.

Besides this, fortune, it would seem, had finally been kind to Malcolm Steadman. Or maybe it had been merciful? After being unemployed for this long Malcolm was starting to give up, so when he was called in for an interview the day before he was stricken with a great elation. He was also totally unprepared. The universe had given him a bone, everything that happened after that was his own fault.

His morning preparing for his interview was in a stark contrast to the one he had prepared for some weeks earlier. Unlike before he was not confident, and time did not seem to be on his side. He shaved quickly and in his haste to get prepared and out the door in time to get to the bus stop, he had forgotten his phone and thus his main source for telling time. It was only now, in his anxiety to get on the bus and away from the shady looking boy that Malcolm realized he was missing it. He watched as the hooligan beside him put on some earbuds and briefly debated whether or not he should ask him for the time.

Malcolm took a deep breath, and decided that his need to know if the bus was late outweighed his fear of the shady looking boy. He gathered up his courage and tapped the boy lightly on the shoulder but was immediately ignored. Rude. Some time passed and Malcolm fought away the urge to let it be and tapped the boy on the shoulder once more. He watched as the boy pulled the earbud closest to Malcolm out of his ear and arrogantly left the other earbud in. "Eh, er... excuse me, do you know what time it is?" Malcolm asked the boy timidly. It was just then that Malcolm realized that the boy looked very uncomfortable and realized now that the youth probably thought Malcolm was creepy. After all, what business did a grown man have talking to a teenager if not for some ulterior motive? This realization seemed suddenly cruel to Malcolm. When had Malcolm departed so far from youth culture that this perception could come to someone so easily? Was Malcolm out of touch with the youth?

The boy answered "It's seven-thirty", and did not look directly at Malcolm. Everything about the boy's posture and body language screamed fear. Malcolm decided to lighten the mood, try and ease the boy's fears and demonstrate that he was not some creepy psychopath. He decided to do this with a joke: "I guess it's about time the bus showed up huh?" the Boy's earbuds were back in his ears and at full blast, he did not hear him.

The joke would not have worked anyway, it would have made Malcolm seem even creepier.

The boy's music came throbbing back and suddenly Malcolm recognized the artist: it was Pink Floyd. The boy was listening to Pink Floyd! Malcolm had first listened to Pink Floyd when he was this boy's age, and at first, this was an exciting development. He had something in common with the boy! Maybe Malcolm was not as out of touch as he had once thought!

Then the existential crisis came.

Malcolm Steadman had sought out a new job about a month ago because he was terribly unhappy, and though he was going in for an interview for a new job today, would that change anything? Regardless if he liked this new job, he needed it now out of necessity. Without it, his savings would run dry and he would likely be out on the streets. This job was in the same field as his previous one, so if he was successful in getting it, he would not be successful in changing his life like he had originally sought. Malcolm would continue to be unhappy. Financially stable again, yes, but unhappy. What was worse was that this was the best he could do.

Malcolm had first heard Pink Floyd's "Dark Side of

the Moon" when he was this shady looking boy's age. He had an entire life ahead of him with all of the potential that implies. What had he done since that was worth bragging about? He was now middle-aged, out of shape, and terribly unhappy. He was constantly unfulfilled and now he was going in for an interview for "more of the same". How much longer would Malcolm live his life like this? The most he had done to "liven" up his life lately was let a puzzle gather dust and buy a toy dinosaur out of a sense of nostalgia! Was nostalgia all he had to look forward to now? Was looking back all he had ahead of him?

There was an opportunity here: Malcolm could not change his past, he could not course correct his life immediately, but he could warn the boy next to him, he could let him know of the dangers of growing old... of growing old and regretting. Like Malcolm years ago this shady looking teenager had an entire life ahead of him. If Malcolm acted, maybe this kid would not be in his shoes now, decades later...

Malcolm turned to the boy now, squared his shoulders at him with intent, and tried to gather up the courage to give the boy a speech that would change his life. The boy, sensing Malcolm's posture, reached into his pocket and grabbed on to something... *a knife?!* Malcolm reeled in horror and took a step back as if he were pushed away by the boy's gaze. Whatever the boy had touched in his pocket stayed there and Malcolm watched as the boy removed both earbuds from his ears and gave him his full attention. This was it. This was the moment that Malcolm would change this scary looking kid's life forever.

Instead, Malcolm stammered his speech and sounded like an idiot as he misquoted his favorite band.

"That line, 'the sun is the same in a relative way but

you're older'? Er, uh no, I meant the line 'ten years have got behind you, no one told you when to run, you missed the starting gun'? That one, the one that goes like that, well... It's true" Malcolm ranted.

Knowing that he had already failed at what he had tried to accomplish, Malcolm took a few seconds to gather his thoughts better. In this time neither he nor the boy spoke, but the awkwardness between them grew to be louder than words.

"I-I was your age when I first heard that line, it was an old song even when I was young, do you understand? I was your age and now... now I'm going in for an interview for a job that is meaningless and I see no way out of it. Every day I realize that more and more that my life has no meaning and I don't know what to do with myself! And what's more, do you know the Irony of it?" The boy shook his head in response.

"The irony is that someone DID tell me when to run, someone warned me about not hearing 'the starting gun' and it was that song. Pink Floyd had warned me all of those years ago and I ignored it! Desperation crept to the forefront of Malcolm's speech as he saw the bus near in the corner of his eye. "I must've heard that song hundreds of times since and it never lit a fire under my ass to change anything. Don't. Be. Me. Don't grow up to be me. I wish someone told me that, but I'm telling you, I'm telling you now, *this is the starting gun.*"

The bus had finally arrived.

"Do something with your life" Malcolm pleaded.

"Cool," said the boy.

The boy let Malcolm get on the bus first. Malcolm sat up front, the boy went to the very back. Before the boy sat, Malcolm eyed him taking a granola bar, the boy's breakfast, out of his pocket. Malcolm laughed to himself as he realized now that the granola bar was "the knife" he had felt so threatened from moments earlier. The bus crept slightly forward and began moving. Neither of them looked at each other the entire ride.

Malcolm wished he had his phone with him. He wanted to listen to Pink Floyd.

15

Was nostalgia all he had to look forward to now? Was looking back all he had ahead of him? The thought had not gone away. He had done his best to repress it, and considering his history with being overwhelmed by existential dread, had actually done a good job at it. Until now.

After his incredibly awkward interactions with the shady looking boy at the bus stop, Malcolm Steadman kept his cool and was able to collect himself before his interview. Though the thought had done its best to demand his attention, he was able to ignore it and excelled at his job interview. Malcolm seemed calm, personable, and most importantly: sane. He was able to answer every question with ease, even as he was playing a sort of whack-a-mole with the sentiment he was trying to ignore. Malcolm was at his best, and it had paid off, he walked away with the job. He walked away with a more secure future, he walked away with a guarantee that he could go on to enjoy the comforts he had become accustomed to. He should have walked away with a sense of success and pride, but the thought was like an infection, and it was spreading. *Was nostalgia all he had to look forward to now?*

Malcolm was on the bus again, this time on his return trip. The sordid and cold atmosphere of the bus burdened his mood and was only broken by the warm and brightly colored fast food container Malcolm had purchased for breakfast. It contained one solitary breakfast burrito and about a dozen hot sauce packets. This was a victory meal, his celebratory feast for accomplishing his goal for the day. It was as disappointing as it was non-perishable: infinitely so. It was even more disappointing that he was unable to eat it on the bus, he could feel it getting cold. It was succumbing to the sordid atmosphere of the bus, just like Malcolm's mood.

After having left his phone at home, Malcolm had nothing to distract him. It was this exact situation that the thought needed to cultivate. *Was looking back all he had ahead of him?* He had no choice now but to consider it. His existential angst from earlier in the day had cropped up like an unwanted weed because of his unfulfilled life, and though it had reached its peak, it had sown the seed for the one that was growing now. Malcolm's most reliable source of happiness was a comforting sense of nostalgia.

Malcolm realized now that nostalgia was a powerful force in his life. Aside from driving him to purchase the plastic dinosaur, it was likely the only reason he had seen any recent movie on the big screen. In fact, *every* movie he had seen in the past decade could be attributed to Nostalgia. Every single title he could think of was either a sequel, a reboot, or a property based off of something he had enjoyed from his childhood. Each movie had characters and plots from comic books he had read, or cartoons he used to watch. Malcolm chose to spend his free time, and his money, on something that he already knew. They were safe. Malcolm was actively shielding himself from something new.

Why not? The new and unknown could be frightening! They could be disappointing! It was just easier to wrap yourself up in a warm memory, one that you knew you could trust, than to let something *new* have the chance to disappoint you. Nostalgia was a for sure win, the unknown is a gamble. Nostalgia was a cheap panacea that kept out anything different, and what scared Malcolm to his utmost core, was that he had willingly, and repetitively, taken it.

With nothing new in his life, would Malcolm spend the rest of it with his head in his past? Nostalgia could be a comfort, but he realized now that it had slowly become a god in his life. It was something that he worshiped and begged for. Whenever he was sad or unsure in his life, it was nostalgia that he had turned to so that he could feel better. Had a bad day? Malcolm would unwind by watching a show he had already seen. Depressed about his lack of a love life? Malcolm would listen to the same cheerful songs he always did. Malcolm was inadvertently idolizing the past to avoid the discomforts of the present. Here was the crux of it: the past? It objectively sucked. The picturesque 1950's that America so loved and that so many wanted to go back to was rampant with segregation laws. The lucrative and prosperous decade that was the 1980's was really filled with an overwhelming fear of nuclear annihilation and an AIDS epidemic. The disenfranchised had less rights than they did now when Malcolm's grandparents were his age. Hell, the disenfranchised had less rights than they did now in Malcolm's short lifetime. Technology, medicine, and even the entertainment he felt so nostalgic for were worse. The only thing the past had over the future, and the only thing that made nostalgia such a powerful sedative was that it was a *known*. But was it worth the price of admission?

By actively worshiping the past, by letting nostalgia

be his security blanket, Malcolm was ensuring that his best days were the ones behind him. He had let the sense of wonderment and adventure about the future be replaced by dread because it was an unknown, and with it he had replaced hope with nostalgia. The bleak and terrible ocean of Wednesdays that he had seen before him in a previous epiphany was suddenly more horrifying as he easily saw himself spending them looking back into the past. Nothing new would happen. Nothing would change, and it was Malcolm's own fault.

His epiphany did not have the same sort of paralyzing effect that the others had. Malcolm did not feel like the earth beneath him had vanished and that he was free-falling helplessly into a vast void of existential terror. No, this time was different. There was an opportunity here. As the bus crept to a stop Malcolm stood and descended off of it with a new sense of guilt for his actions, and he embraced it. He had every reason to feel guilty about letting nostalgia replace hope in his life. It was not existential terror he felt, it was a sense of disappointment that he had so easily given in to fear. He had time to change course, he could embrace the future and make it so that the best days were once again those that were ahead of him. *Was nostalgia all he had to look forward to now? Was looking back all he had ahead of him?* No. Not if he had his way.

Malcolm ate his burrito when he got home. It was the kind he always ordered. It would be the same kind he ordered the next day.

...and the day after that.

16

Tree.

The forest is never quiet. Birds only stop chirping when there is danger.

The amount of time that had gone by since the tree was just a sapling to what it was now, was almost immeasurably long. The sun had chased the moon so many times in the tree's life it was hard to say that anything had changed at all. When it was a seed, it was so minuscule, so vulnerable. There were so many creatures, each infinitely more capable of movement and speed than the seed, and each of them could have collected it up and eaten it. Its life could have ended there, before the moon had a chance to reign the sky. But it didn't. The seed went unnoticed, and the seed gave root.

So slow was the process. To say that the root had "inched" out was inaccurate because that was too quick. The root's speed was painfully slow for any of the creatures above to notice, nor would they have had the time to watch. So short, so brief would they exist, by the time the seed would become a sapling most of them would cease to be. When it broke out of the ground, when it was free to see the sun again, it noticed how lonely it was. There was not another tree here. It was the only one. So it came up with a plan. It would change that.

First, it needed to grow. So, it grew.

The tree began to stretch. Still, it went unnoticed. Creatures that would have eaten it when it was just a seed ignored it now, it had no value to them. So it soaked up the warmth of the sun, gathered and collected its light no matter the weather. The infinite vastness of the sky changed more often and so much more rapidly than the tree. Still it grew.

To the creatures around the tree, it was always there, no more moveable and just as ancient as the mountains. They had no idea that it was once so tiny, so minuscule, but now it was a tower. The tree had finally, after stretching for longer than anything around it had ever lived, become useful to the creatures again. It was noticed. Noticed, but still alone. Birds had nested in the tree, taking refuge in its massive branches. So small were they, so fragile and vulnerable. Like the seed. They were protected in the tree, away from harm and danger. The sound of birds was now constant, and they sang endlessly. Yet the tree was not done growing.

It shed its own seeds now. Most were collected, most were eaten, most did not make it. A few did though. A few started to stretch just like the tree, and they grew into saplings. With time, as the sun chased away the moon again and again, they too became trees, and they too shed seeds.

Still it grew.

A fungus had grown between the tree's roots and reached out to the roots of other trees. A complex hyphal network created by the mycorrhizal fungi connected the tree to what used to be its seeds and it was no longer alone. It could transfer nitrogen, carbon, and even water to its saplings if they suffered. The tree took care of the others, let them grow to be their full potential. No creature above had any idea just how closely the trees were connected, how active they were. The ground had grown darker now as the tree and its brood shadowed it with their great mass. There were so many now. Yet the tree was not done growing.

The forest was so loud now, there was always birds singing. The tree's brood had birds of their own. There was so much life now, yet so much of it was brief. The lives of the creatures around the tree were so infinitesimal. Compared to them, the tree was a god, a creature of massive stature and potential, a being that lived for so long it could be said to have existed forever. This god had given shelter to endless generations of creatures, and even the "waste" of this being created life as it turned carbon into oxygen. It was mighty and it was seemingly endless.

And then the forest was silent. The birds had stopped chirping.

A man cut into the tree, and in no time at all, had cut it down. The tree fell. The god was dead. Its corpse was carried away to a mill. Its brood followed.

Malcolm Steadman held what was now left of the tree, of the old god that once housed more birds in its lifetime than Malcolm had lived in days. The history of it had just occurred to him. It was in Malcolm's hand now, a tiny square of toilet paper, and he wiped his ass with it.

Then he flushed it.

Malcolm Steadman will dial the suicide hotline in 46 days.

The aroma of the port wine felt sweet and heavy as Malcolm Steadman poured it into a glass. He swirled it around merrily and admired its dark color. Setting it down, Malcolm moved on now to his stove where he removed two slices of fried bananas from the heated pan and lovingly placed them on top of his freshly made waffles. His happy stride was closer to that of a dance as he glided without worry and fetched the candied maple bacon strips from his other pan. His whistling was as light as his mood and became a sort of jazz as he drizzled melted peanut butter on top of his breakfast concoction. Malcolm rarely took the time to cook like this and admired his decadent plate with pride. He sat now, with his waffles in front of him, and his port wine back in his hand deliberately facing a blank wall. It was time for his scheduled panic attack.

Yes, *scheduled* panic attack. He was proud of the idea.

If Malcolm Steadman was going to be plagued by his panicked ponderings anyways, why not set aside a specific time for them, why not just get them out of the way? His existential terror had as of late stricken at times that were inconvenient, and now that he was going back to work in a couple of days and had vowed not to let his future be dimmer than his past he could not afford to let them hinder him again. Though he was vaguely aware that scheduling a panic attack into his week would look like the habits of a madman to an observer, he saw no other option. Aside from self-trepanation what else could he do? No, it was better to get them out of the way, to treat them as a chore that needed to be done. Malcolm sipped his wine.

Everything he was doing now was deliberate. All of the conditions for his philosophical freak-outs were there: He was not distracted by his phone, his environment was mundane and boring, and it was time for breakfast (when the majority of his terrors seemed to take place). Yes, the meal and its port wine companion were a little more lavish than he normally had, but why not make an event out of it? If Malcolm was going to schedule a panic attack, he was going to enjoy it. So Malcolm began to eat his favorite comfort food and stared intently at the blank wall. Time passed.

Mr. Steadman will not be successful in his efforts today, as enterprising as they were. This is not to say that he wouldn't have a panic attack that day, no, that would happen in the night, but his scheme to have a controlled one will fail. His breakfast, however, will otherwise be a success, in the sense that he had one. The attack at night will creep up on him where he is most vulnerable...

Malcolm washed down the taste of peanut butter and bananas with the port and started to feel buzzed. Nothing had happened yet, maybe he was concentrating too hard? He felt that there was a lot at stake here in his experiment. His first day at his new job was just a couple of days ahead, and later that week he had a date. Yes, Malcolm had a date! Well, the beginnings of one at the very least. He had first come up with the idea to schedule a panic attack after his old manager texted him to meet for a coffee. Because he was no longer her subordinate and believing that he had purposefully taken a nose dive when they were competing for the same job, she reached out to him. His replies were awkward and embarrassing, the last thing he needed was a frightening epiphany when he went to meet her. It was imperative that he got that out of the way now.

Nothing.

Malcolm had finished his breakfast, he had downed the last bit of wine, and no epiphany came. The main antagonist in his life had not shown when scheduled. He continued to stare at the wall for a little longer, occasionally checking the time nervously. He hoped that his date later that week would not be a repeat of this, him, sitting alone, waiting for something that wouldn't show. Malcolm giggled to himself at the idea that he had been stood up by his existential dread and washed his dishes. At least Breakfast was good.

Peanut butter and bacon, as it turns out, is not good for digestion.

Malcolm will wake up in the middle of the night with a sharp pain in his bowels. He will rush to the toilet and in a sweat will rid his body of his breakfast. He will glance at his toilet paper roll and will ponder the full beginnings of it as a tree. He will flush the toilet with the remains of that tree in shock. It will take him a full hour to go back to sleep as his mind will reel in horror of the panic attack that finally came.

He will feel relief moments before succumbing to sleep. Whether or not the panic came when he wanted it to, it was now out of the way. He could go on to his first day at work, and later his date without worry.

Malcolm, is often wrong, and unaware of the countdown.

18

Red Flag.

Malcolm Steadman will dial the suicide hotline in 41 days.

The combined echolalia in Karen's row as other customer service reps recited problems back to their customers faded and dulled as she logged on and put on her headset and the "waiting music" took hold. Karen had a complicated relationship with the waiting music. It could be a nice reprieve, a chance for her to catch her breath and center herself after a difficult call, or it could be an incredible vexation that was worse than the mindless echolalia that surrounded her. Currently it was playing an instrumental to an early Brittany Spears song. This was *not* a moment when the song became a reprieve.

The row that she sat in at the call center seemed like an endless distance of grey growing in either direction beside her. She did not have her own desk. They all sat at the same super long desk, a massive piece of particle board that stretched the entire aisle. Each Customer

Service Representative was partitioned off from the rest by plastic walls covered in a grey carpet. These partitions were only about two and a half feet apart, and between them were old CRT monitors, the massive beige kind that weighed ten pounds and took up the majority of the partitioned space. The cold glow of the monitor and its low resolution was the closest thing to the sun that Karen would see for eight hours. Stuck to the bottom face of the monitor was a bright pink sticky note with the solitary word "Brazil" written on it, a reference to Karen's favorite movie by Terry Gilliam. This was the most that she could do to protest her job and its atmosphere and she giggled to herself now as she realized that Terry Gilliam got the future wrong. It wasn't bleak enough.

The music came to an abrupt end as she was connected with a customer, in a few moments Karen would hear the customer's asinine complaint and she would likely be berated and yelled at for conditions she had no control over. She heard the telephone line click and asked for the customer's phone number, when she typed it in a file was brought up on the customer. His name was Malcolm Steadman, and his file was **extensive**.

"What can I do for you today Mr. Steadman?" Karen asked as half a dozen other reps mindlessly parroted the same but with different names. She skimmed over the customer's notes as he spoke. Each note carried with it a date, the problem, and the name of the rep who entered the note. Malcolm Steadman had called them *seven times* in the span of just two weeks, and there was a common theme among each call. She was able to read two of them.

- *-3.22:*
- *customer called in to complain about slow*

connection and flashing blue light on modem. care documents have nothing on such light, customer ranted on about various existential crisis and was upset about carbon :(smh customer hung up after issue resolved self. -Michelle F.

- *-3.24:*
- *Customer claims internet service has slowed. As I referred to care documents customer declared that dinosaur toys were "a perverse monument to the massive amount of time and life it contained in its form", seemed more animated and worried about that than he did his connection. -Lucas D.*

"The blue light, uh, just won't stop flashing" Malcolm informed her. Karen was not prepared to deal with a crazy person.

"let's see what we can do about that" she responded and tried to flag Michelle, who sat behind her in the row, over to her screen. She was unsuccessful. "I see you have had this problem in the past" Karen continued "give me just a moment to look over your notes".

- *-3.27*
- *customer referred to blue lights flashing which dont exist and was very worried about dying or something -Ben B.*

- *-4.1*
- *Malcolm called in again about fake problems. Notified management. This time he was upset about a dream he had about a man trying to kill his neighbor and what that meant about his own fleeting mortality. Terminated call. -Cyntia C.*

Though Karen had been trying urgently to get Michelle's attention, she had to stay silent so that the customer would not hear her, and had failed to do so again. Malcolm had not skipped a beat and was currently describing a date he had gone on with a former manager of his, or at least he *thought* it was a

date. Karen rolled her eyes at the details of it.
- *-4.2*
- *Customer called in AGAIN about flashing lights. This time he asked me if Pink Floyd ever made me question reality. Is this guy high? I offered to send out a technician to look at his modem but the customer terminated the call early. - Hannah Q.*

Michelle had finally noticed Karen and looked at her with a puzzled expression. Karen muted her end as Malcolm droned on about his date, and asked Michelle in a hushed tone "did you talk to this guy?" Michelle looked at the monitor and the notes as Malcolm continued on about how he had accidentally spilled his coffee, something that he was apparently doing all of the time. Michelle rolled her eyes and mouthed the words "yes, he is crazy". She then mimed her finger cutting her throat, and the message to Karen was clear: "end the call". Karen turned back to her desk and continued reading as Malcolm's mood seemed to turn sour.

- *-4.3*
- *customer complained about blue light again, read previous notes and tried to flag down a manager, see how I should proceed. customer seemed upset about toilet paper? smh - Michelle F.*

Malcolm was ranting about how the puddle of stained coffee spill had some cream that was not completely mixed in, and that it reminded him of our spiral galaxy, The Milky Way. He continued ranting that at that moment he realized that the formation of our universe, the big bang, was akin to the random act of him dropping his coffee, and that made him feel like life was meaningless.

Karen listened on.

The rest of Malcolm's date was soiled from that instant. As hard as he tried to get over the awkwardness of it, the realization that the universe was arbitrary had ruined his mood, and there was a moment, though he didn't know how long, that he was catatonic from it. "It could have been anywhere from a minute to ten, I have no idea, but my former manager was not happy about it" Malcolm stated. "She thought I was disinterested, that I was making a big ordeal over nothing" he continued. *This man*, Karen thought, *has some serious issues*.

- *-4.3*
- *looks like this guy called in this morning. He asked me if I liked my job, said he got a new one and that was a problem? He's either prank calling us or needs a therapist. He has refused to allow a technician over and the problem is not one that exist with that model of modem. RED FLAG. -Sr. Floor Manager, Vernan H.*

Red Flag. It meant do not engage, terminate the call when you get it.

"I don't know, I guess I put a lot of pressure on myself. Nothing has gone right" Malcolm said after a pause. "I got a new job, I quit my old one because I didn't like it... didn't like her. I wanted to change my life. I got a new job and I like it, I REALLY like it, do you understand? But it's exactly like my old job. Nothing has changed". Karen listened on, now impatiently. Malcolm continued to rant on, "So I have this date with my old manager, which is something I thought would never happen. We didn't get along 'till she was no longer my manager and I have been lonely and-" Karen couldn't wait any longer, something had been bothering her.

"Sir" she interrupted "Sir what is her name? You keep calling her your old manager. What is her name?" There was a long and silent pause on the other end. "Sir?" Karen asked.

The fear and disappointment in Malcolm's voice spoke louder than his actual volume "I'm... I'm doing it again. I dehumanized her because of her title and I..." Whatever was going on the other end of the phone, Karen was tired of listening. The "Red Flag" gave her permission to hang up, should she take advantage of it? She hesitated, considered that this may be Malcolm's only outlet to talk about his problems. Some people see a therapist, others hire sex workers and just talk. Some people talk to their priests, others their spouse. Malcolm, it appeared, talked to customer service. The other end was silent now, supposedly whatever had happened to him during his date was happening now. There was nothing Karen could do for him now. Whatever problems this man was dealing with, he was going to have to deal with them alone. Karen terminated the call and wrote:

- *-4.4*
- *Malcolm called in again. Terminated call. -Karen W.*

After hesitating for a moment, Karen then wrote "RED FLAG" and queued it to the top of the notes.

The Brittany Spears Instrumental that played over the phone now was a nice reprieve.

Malcolm Steadman will dial the suicide hotline in 34 days.

He could hear the infernal machine, he could hear it ticking away, but he knew he could not look at it. *No matter what happens*, Malcolm thought, *don't look at the clock. Don't look at the clock.*

He could feel it creeping up on him, he knew that it was just around the corner... and there was nothing he could do about it. Malcolm Steadman would once again fall prey to boredom, to listlessness. Malcolm would succumb to the mundane, and existential despair would swallow him whole.

Malcolm Steadman was especially vulnerable today. He had extra time to kill before work, something that took him completely off guard. He had been successful in filling his schedule up to the brim, a tactic that not only would let him earn more money (something he desperately needed after being unemployed for so long) and avoid having time to think. It was spare time that was his enemy, and now he had an extra hour in his day. Every weekday except for today, Malcolm had to be at work at eight in the morning, something he had forgotten when setting his alarm, and now he had woken up too early.

Don't look at the clock. Don't think about the time you have.

Since he started work, save for the weekend, Malcolm had been skipping breakfast. His schedule was that tight, and save for an extremely embarrassing and failed outing, he was content. Content, not happy. Outing, not *date*.

It was embarrassing that he thought it was a date.

Malcolm popped in some bread into his toaster, and he did his best to ignore the quaint, yet antagonizing clock on his wall. He considered picking up his phone because it had EVERY distraction known to man, but remembered that it had a very prominent clock on it. He was absolutely sure that the terror that was stalking him, the epiphany that would seize him and ruin him, would be "time" today. Time was his greatest enemy. Any minute now he would consider the entire concept of time and a panic attack would drown out what little contentedness he had left. But he was wrong. The real villain, as always, was the one he least suspected.

Don't look at the clock.

His toast popped.

Malcolm moved his toast tentatively over to his table and slowly ate it, being sure to focus more on the noise of it crunching in his mouth than that of his clock ticking away. There was another reason why he was avoiding his phone, a reason besides its clock that was keeping him from submerging himself in the screen's cold glow: embarrassment. Embarrassment and guilt.

Malcolm was up late last night, and he was drinking, and he did the thing everyone should not do when a failed and awkward "date" was on their mind: He drunk texted Maggie.

His old manager's name was Maggie. He would never refer to her as his old manager again.

Malcolm could not bear to look at what he wrote. He remembered little of it, but he knew it could not be good. Drunk texts were never good. What's worse? What if she responded? Their "date" was one of the most awkward things Malcolm had ever put himself through, and the fact that he had put so much meaning on getting coffee was alarming. Was he so lonely, so desperate for companionship, that he blindly thought he was going out on a date with someone who, only month's earlier, he had despised? Sure, they had great rapport and had much in common during their competing interview, but was that enough to switch gears from loathing to crush? Apparently so.

It was not the panic attack that did him in during his "date". After he had spilled his coffee, after he had a panic attack centering around the whole of creation, Malcolm poured his heart out. That's what was *embarrassing*. After having built the "date" up in his mind so much, the pressure had finally got to him. He gushed and nearly cried. He admitted that he just wanted it to go well, that if it didn't he had no idea when he would get another chance with the opposite sex. He admitted that it had been so long since he had any amount of intimacy with anyone that he would be relieved to just simply be touched again. The embarrassment was bad. Nagasaki bad.

Malcolm desperately missed human touch. He should have been thinking about the clock.

Of course, he pondered, *touch was impossible*. Malcolm

was an immense pile of matter. An amalgamation of atoms that were, at the base of everything, not connected, but just within close approximation of each other. Atoms under normal, non-extreme circumstances, never touch. These infinitesimally tiny particles that everything is made up of, cannot meet. They must never collide or else a REAL Nagasaki will rip everything around it asunder. Touch, and there would be nothing but nuclear fire, and seeing that Malcolm's life was not one nuclear fire after another, did this mean that he had not ever actually touched anything? Had Malcolm never really been touched?

He *really* should have been thinking about time instead.

Everyone he loved, everyone Malcolm ever had physical contact with, had never actually touched him. Every reassuring hug, every friendly pat on the back, every kiss, every single moment he clutched a naked lover close to him and shared their warmth before succumbing to sleep, did those moments only exist in his mind? *Damn* the fact that he had not been touched longer than any healthy person should, had he, *according to physics*, **never been touched at all?**

His mother, his friends, his lovers and enemies, even his old dogs. All of that intimacy was an illusion.

Malcolm let out an involuntary and pathetic sounding squeal of desperation and fear. He sat in his chair, seized by his philosophical hysteria, and sat in silence. He had been attacked by his enemy despite his efforts to avoid it. He was so convinced that the clock would be the trigger that he…

THE CLOCK! Malcolm had finally looked at the clock, and to his horror saw that it was now much later than he had thought it was.

Malcolm Steadman was late for work. He should have looked at the clock.

After grabbing his coat, and actively trying to ignore the fact that despite him feeling it in his hands there was no physical contact at the smallest level, Malcolm sprinted out the door. He left his toast.
He would eat it in shame when he got home. It will be as stale as his temperament.

There was a response on his phone.

Malcolm Steadman will dial the suicide hotline in 27 days.

His knuckles white, and his sweat cold, Malcolm Steadman gripped the chocolate toaster strudel in front of him as if it were a neck he was trying to strangle. He watched, almost paralyzed as it crumbled into pieces and fell to his kitchen floor like grains of sand in an hour-glass. It was done. *All of those poor giraffes*, he thought helplessly, *gone, **forever.***

His mental crisis was over, and though his breakfast was sacrificed in the process, he was relieved that he was done with it. He could go about the rest of his day knowing that he would not be assaulted by another epiphany. Relieved, but saddened. He could never eat chocolate again. *All of those poor giraffes*, he thought again. At least the worst part of his day was over. Malcolm Steadman looked down at his smartphone to check the time. It was seven 'o clock. His attacks were getting longer, and though this last one had gone on for twenty minutes, he still had time to get to work. He ignored the red numbered notification at the corner of his texting app and put away his phone.

Maggie.

The notification had been there for a week, the text had been left unopened. He did not dare to read it, he was still far too afraid of its consequences.

Convinced that he could go about the rest of his day without the threat of his existential terror gripping him, Malcolm walked to the bus station, and he went to work. He did not feel invincible, but he did feel safe.

No amount of feeling safe can help you when you are your own worst enemy.

As far as his coworkers knew, Malcolm was an ordinary, well put together every-man. To his coworkers, Malcolm was as normal as one could possibly be, and Malcolm aimed to keep it that way. When asked how his mornings went, Malcolm lied. He could never tell them that he had just spent his morning physically stricken with horror thinking about the obvious correlation between the darkness of chocolate and the mortality rate of giraffes. No, even if that were explained from the beginning, it would sound too absurd. Too abnormal. Instead he would just say that he read the news off of his phone. The epiphany he had about oil after buying a toy dinosaur? No one would understand. No, he went jogging, he would say. Had he been fretting about the impossibility of being touched on a particle level? Of course not, he was on his social media page that whole morning looking at pictures of puppies.

Malcolm. Was. Normal. There was nothing to see here. The only people who knew differently were strangers working for his internet provider...

Until today.

Today, he felt safe from his existential terror, believing that if he had one in a day that he would not have to deal with another. This notion was the cornerstone to his earlier plotting when he tried to schedule time in for a panic attack. These terrible epiphanies, weren't they just like going to the dentist? A lot of pain at first, but it was one and done, right?

No.

Malcolm chatted with a co-worker, and instead of telling them that he had once had a philosophical crisis because he forgot to plug his toaster in, lied about being a part of an online fantasy sports league. Instead of admitting that the lifespan of carbon made him anxious and that he couldn't eat toast without thinking about the whole of creation and its potential energy being wasted on reality television, he lied about all of the golf that he didn't play. Malcolm's coworker laughed politely at all of Malcolm's cheesy jokes and regarded Malcolm as a normal guy. Malcolm's coworker had no idea that the days Malcolm came in sweaty were due to him constantly reassessing reality. He just thought Malcolm liked to jog.

It was time to clock in, to get to work, and both men wrapped up their conversation and ended their simple pleasantries. "Gotta get to the 'ol grinder," his coworker said in jest, "time is money".

Time is money. Time IS money. Malcolm contemplated it. He had heard the saying dozens, if not hundreds of times, and though he knew its correlation, did he fully understand its meaning? *Time. Is. Money.* The phrase kept repeating itself like a mad mantra. His money, was his time.

Each hour that Malcolm worked, each minute that he spent doing his job, was traded for in dollars and cents. Money was not just a necessity to buy the food and shelter that he needed, it was an actual *measurement* of his time. When Malcolm handed over a five dollar bill for his coffee in the morning, that bill represented him being here at work. When Malcolm Steadman bought the plastic dinosaur, that was him trading in an hour of his mortal life. An hour that he would never, EVER get back.

Malcolm was trading in a finite amount of time to be spent here, doing something he did not like and felt was unfulfilling, for a number. Just a number. He could not trade in his time forever, someday Malcolm Steadman was going to die, and when he did, what would he have spent his time on? Suddenly his money seemed all the more precious to him, suddenly he felt the gravity of spending it on trivial things. Malcolm had spent a portion of his finite life on a toy dinosaur because it made him nostalgic for his childhood, a toy that, at the end of the day had made him miserable and that was useless. *What hour was that?* He wondered. Which specific moment had he given away for that failed escapade? Did it matter? He suddenly saw himself aging before him, every dollar representing a wrinkle on his face, every swipe of his debit card a grey hair.

The problem wasn't simply that Malcolm was earning his money doing something he hated. Hell, the problem wasn't even that someone else's mortality was arbitrarily worth more than his own if he considered that others got paid more. The problem was what he chose to trade in his mortality for, the things that he bought. Was the fast-food breakfast really worth whatever moment he had to spend at his job? Was that beer he bought the other night a fair trade for something as valuable, and scarce, as his mortality? Malcolm knew, not suspected, but *knew* that most of the things he owned were either consumable or petty in nature. Malcolm was bad with money, and therefore bad with time. When he died, he would leave behind him monuments to his time, each belonging representing him doing something he didn't want to do. Malcolm's whole life could be represented by his cheesy, tacky possessions.

His sofa? That represented three weeks of his life. His Tupperware? An hour that he could have spent painting. Every single beer that he bought, consumed, and abused to waste even more time? Months scattered across his life that he could have used learning a new language. All of these things, they would be the real testament to Malcolm's life. No matter how shiny his epitaph, no matter how well written his obituary, the real representation of how Malcolm spent his time were inanimate things that he bought mostly on impulse, and didn't understand why he wanted them after he had them.

Something was wrong. A wall of concerned faces was staring at him. Malcolm had not moved for ten whole minutes, and his coworkers had noticed.

"Are you okay?" one of his coworkers had asked, "what's wrong?"

"Is he having a seizure? You know they don't always shake like they do in the movies?" another offered.

"Malcolm, Malcolm can you hear me what's wrong? Why are you staring into space like that?" a Coworker asked looking grim. The same coworker that uttered "time is money". Malcolm, still in a state of shock, and existential hysteria, told him the truth for the first time since he had met him.

"I can't be here!" Malcolm screamed. "Time is money! Time is money don't you see?" Malcolm pointed angrily at the clock. "No one should be here! We are all going to die, and our sofas are going to make us look stupid. ALL OF OUR SOFAS WILL MAKE US LOOK STUPID IN THE END! DON'T YOU SEE?!"

Malcolm's coworker backed away from him slowly, cautiously. Each step was soft so as not to agitate him. Malcolm watched in horror as his coworker did this, realizing now that his coworker thought Malcolm was a threat. He watched as the concerned faces switched from that of empathy, to that of fear. He noticed now, for the first time, that he had been holding a pen tightly as if it were a knife. "Our, our sofas...they are gonna... don't look at me like that I didn't... they, the sofas..." Malcolm muttered while hot tears streaked down his helpless face. His hand went limp, and let the pen fall impotently to the floor. "...our sofas..."

Malcolm knew that he was in the wrong, that he was the villain here, but he also knew that now that the facade was broken, now that they all knew that he was mad as a hatter, that there was no going back. There was no way that he wasn't going to be fired now.

"I'll ah, I'll just go now, I'm sorry. I've ah, I do this a lot don't worry" he sputtered in admittance. "I've never jogged a day in my life, I am not a part of some stupid fantasy league, and most everything I say about myself is a lie" Malcolm continued. There was nothing but silence in return. Malcolm's hands were shaking.

"I fucking *hate* jogging" Malcolm offered to the silence.

Malcolm Steadman left his former workplace as astonished and fearful as he left his former co-workers. He was filled with instant regret. Malcolm trekked home in silence stunned at what had just happened. He would not regain his faculties for some time, and the horror at what he had just done would not hit him for some hours.

When Malcolm got home, he saw the pile of toaster strudel that he had strangled to dust earlier that morning. There on his floor was a physical reminder that everything was NOT okay. He swept it up, and now that he was back where he had started his day, decided to finally read Maggie's text. It was lengthy, but the final sentence in it read:

"I think you should see someone. You need someone to talk to about this."

21

Her message read "I think you should see someone," so instead, Malcolm drank. Her message read "You need someone to talk to about this," so instead Malcolm got shit-faced, three sheets to the wind, under the table, forgot his own name DRUNK. His face is currently pressed against his cold kitchen floor.

Malcolm has been awake for a good quarter of the hour, he just hasn't moved. Malcolm was not participating today. If the world wanted to be cruel, to be meaningless and absurd, let it, it just had to do so without him.

Not all of this drinking was mere self-pity, no, that was only about half of his reasons to get drunk. The other half was this: if Malcolm's misery was caused by his constant existential dread, if all of his woes were caused by him thinking too much, he would simply drink himself stupid. "Ya can't think if all ya do is-is drink!" Malcolm declared belligerently to the empty air around him as he slowly sat up. He had expected to wake up hungover, but fortune favored him, he woke up still drunk... but not drunk enough.

Malcolm's kitchen was damp and sordid. The smell of warm beer hung over the room with a scent so foul it had integrity. Empty beer cans, now robbed of their contents, had found a new purpose as being homes to flies. There was no organization to this madness, but there was a method: never stop drinking.

"Breakfast of champions!" Malcolm decreed to nobody as he opened a warm beer and drank it with a sad urgency. He was still not drunk enough, he could feel the wheels in his head slowly start to turn as his punished liver filtered out the poison in him. But that was it. There was no more beer. The "party" was over.

Malcolm knew ahead of time that he could only escape to the hazy comfort of inebriation for only so long. At some point, Malcolm knew that he would have to face his tribulations. He knew that he would have to be sober, that he would need to send out his resumé and pray to the gods he did not believe in that he would get another job. He knew all of this ahead of time, he just wasn't ready for that to happen now.

Malcolm sat at his kitchen table, clutching the can of beer near to him for comfort, and slowly took in the self-made horror around him. He had been living in filth for days, and he had been living in it in desperation. Alcohol, though a temporary solution, was the only one that worked to keep himself out of his own mind, assuming he was drunk enough. He is not drunk enough. Alcohol was not the first panacea he reached for after his "episode" at his now former job. The first thing Malcolm reached for was his phone.

He had no idea just how much of a crutch customer service was to him until they started hanging up. He had no idea just how cathartic talking to someone could be, then suddenly it was no longer an option. He had abused his internet provider's customer service line so often that they cut him off. Her message read "I think you should see someone. You need someone to talk to about this" but Malcolm had no one to talk to. He had no friends that were close to him, and he had successfully alienated everyone he had built any rapport with after his "episode". So, Malcolm Steadman paid for his rent ahead of time, spent an offensive amount of money on the cheapest beer and whiskey, and spent the next week on a bender that would make Henry Chinaski feel self-conscious.

Malcolm sat his beer down on the table and noticed that it felt sticky with drying beer. It also felt... bumpy, almost textured. He ignored it. He was not ready to snap back into reality yet. He was not ready to deal with his life.

Shame wafted to Malcolm's mind, he could not decide if it was competing with the acrid smell of stale beer, or if it was complemented and enhanced by it. Reality and its weight was winning, Malcolm would need many more drinks to make it past being a depressed drunk and back into the safe sanctuary of utter delirium. Malcolm picked up his last beer and drank the rest of it slowly, trying his best to enjoy the nectar that kept himself from responsibility for the week, and did his best not to think about the week ahead of him.

He set his empty can back onto the sticky surface of his table and noticed then just why it felt so bumpy, so textured. Laid out on the whole of the table was a stained, but complete, jig-saw puzzle.

Goddammit.

He had done it again. HE HAD DONE IT AGAIN! In his blacked-out state, Malcolm Steadman completed another puzzle without the consent of his higher functions.

Malcolm did not curl into a fetal position, he did not openly weep and lament as he had an existential panic attack. Though his previous fears about free will being an illusion seemed to be confirmed once more before him, Malcolm laughed. Malcolm laughed harder than he had in a very long time.

He also laughed, for a very long time.

When the mania had passed, Mr. Steadman let out a long sigh. *My life*, he thought to himself, *is so damn funny*.

So. Damn. Funny.

Malcolm Steadman will dial the suicide hotline in 20 days.

I am nothing but a shadow, thought Malcolm. Malcolm is freaking out, needlessly might I add. *Not just a shadow*, he continued, *but a shadow* **puppet**. For the record, Malcolm has been completely sober for over a week. This was not the fretting of the inebriated, no, this was the anxiety of the mad.

After purchasing a cheap fast food burrito (cheap is all he an afford now) Malcolm Steadman trekked back to his lonely apartment to stay the integrity of his isolation. Though he was starved for conversation, and though he needed the catharsis of talking to someone, Malcolm was worried that he would have another public freakout. With this in mind, Malcolm limited the time he had around people. He had no positive influence on anyone anyways. How wrong he is. Elsewhere the boy Malcolm crept out at the bus stop has just downloaded a copy of Pink Floyd's Dark Side of the Moon.

Elsewhere Karen, the customer service representative for Malcolm's internet provider is going back through her old notes on Malcolm's account.

Back at his apartment, Malcolm's mind began to wander. Anxiety and dread filled his mind and he prepared for it to spill over. Gone were the days Malcolm tried to combat or avoid his existential terror.

Gone too were the days he tried to force it. His existential terror would happen when it wanted to, and without his permission. He was not at peace with this, but he **was** resigned to it.

Watching the cardboard fast food container that his food was held in, Malcolm Steadman spied the shadow that it cast onto his wall. His anxiety was almost to the brim. He knew it was coming.

Malcolm is needlessly freaking out.

When light bounces off a solid three-dimensional object, like Malcolm's fast food box, a two-dimensional shadow is cast onto a plane, like Malcolm's wall. Thus, the shadow of the box is a square. Malcolm relaxed a little, even if he knew it was in vain. Simple third grade science was not going to set him off into an existential abyss, right?

Of course it will.

Elsewhere the boy packs his glass pipe with weed stolen from his parents.

Elsewhere Karen takes a deep sigh as "waiting music" plays over her headset.

Malcolm Relaxes.

The higher dimension analog to a line is a square. The higher dimension analog to a square is a box. The higher dimension analog to a box is a tesseract, the super cube. Malcolm contemplated this with the same hesitation and expectation one has when they are sure that they are going to be hit in the face. If higher dimensional objects like a tesseract exist, if physical objects can manifest in a fourth dimension, what shadows do *they* cast? If light bounces off of a tesseract, does it cast a three-dimensional shadow? If a box cast a square shadow, would a tesseract cast a cubed shadow? Malcolm flinched. *IT,* was coming.

Because no one can perceive of a fourth dimensional object in its natural state, if they did exist no one could see them. They could view their shadows, however. Could the world around Malcolm be a number of shadows to objects of a higher dimension? Malcolm swallowed nervously. *Could I be a shadow of one of these objects?* Malcolm posited. Then it hit him.

Malcolm conceived that he was a shadow puppet cast by a being beyond his perceptions or understanding, unaware of his exact nature and incapable of understanding it if he was. *I am nothing but a shadow, and not just a shadow, but a shadow **puppet**.* Again, for the record, Malcolm is perfectly sober, if not a little mad.

The cruelty of the concept bothered him most. It was not the fact that he now saw himself as a shadow to a non-euclidean super object that bothered him. What bothered him was that if he was one of these objects, if he was truly a hologram controlled by something outside of his perception and understanding, he was an unhappy hologram. He was a sad shadow puppet. The cruelty was that while he chose to cast a happy dog or a soaring eagle onto his wall when he made shadow puppets, a higher being was casting a sad, lonely, broken man haunted by epiphanies that were bleak and that he did not understand. He imagined fourth dimensional super beings mixing their fourth dimensional analogs of hands into shapes. These beings would laugh and point as one of them made a "Malcolm", his whole life appearing to them in an instant. So sad and confused. So funny.

It was hard to say even for Malcolm whether he believed this was the case or not, but his feelings about it were real, even if the scenario was absurd.

Malcolm felt useless, he felt pointless. He could not make sense of himself or the world around him, let alone make sense of something *more* than him. Malcolm freaked out needlessly. With his existential terror behind him, with his "episode" of geometric nihilism past, Malcolm Steadman felt reaffirmed in his belief that he had no positive influence on anyone.

Elsewhere, the boy lit up his pipe and put on some ear buds. The boy pressed play and for the first time in his life he would listen to Pink Floyd, a band unintentionally recommended to him by Malcolm. It would blow his god damn mind.

Elsewhere, Karen checks her old notes on Malcolm's account during a lull in calls. She will disapprove of how callous and robotic she treated a man losing his mind and clearly in need of someone to talk to.

The boy, after hearing the album all the way through for the second time in this one sitting, will start to pursue philosophy. His life will forever be changed and enriched as he earns a PhD in Philosophy. He will also be in tons of student debt and will look back at his favorite album as being a bit pretentious, but he will be fulfilled.

Karen will realize that she hated solving the shallow problems of the customers that she talks to. She will realize that she has a real opportunity to help people and will decide, after reading her notes and looking casually to her post-it note that reads "Brazil", that she will go back to school to become a therapist. Karen will leave her work feeling guilty for ignoring Malcolm's plea, but she will have her head up high as she applies to community college.

Malcolm does not give himself enough credit. Though terrifying, these epiphanies had lessons. Use your time wisely. Don't objectify people with labels. Do something virtuous.

Elsewhere, Maggie is far less stressed out and enjoys her new job.

Malcolm was better than he perceived of himself. Malcolm has learned more than he will ever give himself credit for. Too much nostalgia can be an empty panacea. Don't look forward to someone's misfortune and pain. Something about giraffes.

Malcolm finished his breakfast.

Thirteen days are left.

Malcolm Steadman will dial the suicide hotline in 6 days.

The far away threat that Malcolm Steadman would be out on the streets was suddenly within view. With no job, and his savings in the double digits, the fear of becoming homeless was very real. This threat definitely weighed on his anxiety, yet it was somehow muted. The existential panic attacks were almost daily now, and the more often they happened the less a "real problem" seemed to matter. In perspective, what was being homeless compared to the vast cold and unfeeling emptiness of space? What was his health in the face of reality's stark and harsh absurdities?

Did Malcolm not care that he was in danger of losing his apartment because he was mad as a hatter, or had he finally gained a sense of perspective? *The line between genius and madman*, Malcolm thought, *is a very thin one.*

Malcolm Steadman is not a genius.

Since Malcolm's "episode", he spent a week spending money he could not spend getting belligerently drunk. He spent the next week sending out his resumé to anyone who would take it, sure, but he also isolated himself from humanity which assured that any call he did get about a job ended with him sounding awkward and desperate. This last week? This last week was *terrible*.

Epiphany after epiphany assaulted Mr. Steadman's frail psyche. Any moment spent not doing anything was an invitation for another wave of these high-powered crises to ravage his mind as if they were coked up bears surviving on nothing but salt. When they were done and had passed, Malcolm often felt incredibly drained. he was having heart palpitations, and breathing was something that was either very hard to do, or something he forgot to do entirely. Malcolm Steadman could find himself out on the streets with nowhere to go, but did that matter if one of these epiphanies could give him a heart attack?

If an inactive moment was all that was needed to be vulnerable, Malcolm did not plan on being inactive. For the fourth day in a row he sat cross-legged on his cold kitchen floor slowly trying to piece together a massive jigsaw puzzle. The same puzzle he had completed blackout drunk. Twice. The fact that he did not need the ever-present and oddly incessant roll of commentary that was consciousness to finish the puzzle terrified him. The fact that he was **better** at assembling a puzzle without it was even worse. Not only was his ego and self-aware nature not necessary, *it was in the way*.

Would Malcolm be happier without it?

No. That was a silly question, "Malcolm" would cease to be. Happiness is a part of consciousness. An end to himself would be an end to happiness.

It would also be an end to his misery.

Malcolm picked up a piece of the puzzle and laid it carefully down into place.

He was miserable.

The puzzle before him was slowly taking form. He had carefully and meticulously built up a border with the edge pieces, laying a foundation for the rest of the pieces to snap together. With this new piece where it needed to be, he noticed an obvious place for another. Malcolm laid the next piece into its spot.
His misery could end.
Though it was originally aesthetically pleasing, the puzzle had been through much. Like Malcolm. It had been violently kicked to pieces and now had dirty boot prints scattered throughout. Random rings of beer stains from the bottom of a bottle peppered the pieces like a pox. Colors were muted and slightly washed as Malcolm inevitably spilled his coffee on it. Layers of violence and strife abused the once cheery picture. The work that was being done now was less about piecing the puzzle's original picture together, and was more about finding which grungy and sticky stain fit into the next. What was on the floor now only looked nice because the bright rays of sun pouring through the kitchen window created a bright glare on it, and thus much of it could barely be seen. Malcolm knew the strife was still there. He snapped in another piece.

His strife could end.

Malcolm was not aware of the Greek concept of eudaimonia, and had never read anything by Susan Wolfe. Having active engagement in projects of worth was not something that was on his mind, and he was unaware of the massive amount of philosophy written that suggested that his current project was virtuous or could make him happy. Aside from *definitely* having a panic attack about it, Malcolm would have scoffed and laughed bitterly at the thought of it. He had originally bought the puzzle as a futile attempt to end boredom and appear to be more interesting. What it had become was a symbol of his feverish and desperate mind and he now had to piece it back together, one stained broken piece at a time.

This puzzle represented not only Malcolm's actions, but also his sanity.

Malcolm laid another piece down. It took him a moment to realize that his train of thought should have bothered him more. Any other day, this would be the crescendo to his existential terror and Malcolm would be paralyzed by it. Now? He was okay. Malcolm was fine. A sense of celebration was mired by a nagging feeling that this was only because Malcolm was tapped out. There was no panic attack because there was simply no energy for. It seems that Malcolm's tyrannical epiphany was countered by his deep unrelenting depression. Hooray.

There was his answer. Malcolm could either live moment to moment on a raw nerve fearful of his next philosophical discovery, or he could be unresponsive from a debilitating depression. Choices.

Malcolm picked out the final piece. Without a sense of victory or pomp he placed the final jigsaw piece into the rest and completed the portrait. Every dirty footprint, every beer stain that smelled like rotten yeast, every scattershot of muted color strained by coffee, they were together now.

He stood up now, his unused knees creaking under the burden of his weight. Malcolm felt a psychosomatic need to dust himself off though their was no dirt on him. He just felt like it was something people did when they finished something. For the first time the puzzle was completed while he was lucid, and thus had lost its allure. Though excitement was not on the menu, Malcolm briefly admired the grungy portrait beneath him.

It was a large photo of bacon and eggs.

Looks like Malcolm forgot to eat.

24

day zero.

Malcolm was thinking clearly. Clearly, Malcolm was thinking, and thinking clearly came with clearly thinking. Malcolm was thinking.

Everything is okay. Nothing is wrong with Malcolm and everything is going to be fine.

Malcolm was thinking clearly. It really was a great idea.

Malcolm's breakfast looked incredibly alluring as steam rose from the freshly cooked scrambled eggs and bacon. This pairing of food was a normal breakfast, if not *the most normal* breakfast, and Malcolm was perfectly normal. Adding Tabasco sauce on his eggs was a popular thing to do and though his third cup of coffee might be excessive plenty of people needed an extra kick to start their day. The whiskey in the coffee just meant that, aside from being your everyday average person, Malcolm Steadman was also fun! He was unemployed, a little bit of day drinking was okay. Malcolm was having fun!

Malcolm was decidedly not having fun.

Feeling intensely self-aware, Malcolm ate his breakfast quickly, intending to get the task over with so that he could move on to the rest of his day. Normal people did things with their day and he had every intention of being a productive member of society in spite of having no job. As soon as he could figure out what that productive thing was.

For a time, Malcolm considered walking the streets and keeping an eye out for any "Help Wanted" signs that might be loosely cradled in a window. This idea ended quickly though. Sure, he needed a job, but he was also incredibly unsocialized. The last person Malcolm interacted with for any length of time was the liquor store clerk when Malcolm decided to spend a week binge drinking. He had easily been alone and without human contact for weeks now, going out in public to look for a job would be disastrous. The simple abstract idea of him exchanging eye contact made him flinch. If only he could go back to his "old ways".

Malcolm Steadman was perfectly normal so the very idea that his attitude towards calling customer service was akin to an old drug addict bargaining for their fix did not seem out-of-place. No, that was a perfectly normal disposition. It had to be. Malcolm was normal.

Though he would never admit it to someone in person, Malcolm greatly missed the satisfaction and validation he felt after calling customer service, and calling them now would help to socialize him and ease his anxiety. He knew that if he could only call his precious hotline, he could easily go outside and look for a job without being so self-conscious. This was no longer an option, however. His go to hotline, his internet provider's customer service, had cut him off. A call would either end immediately, or it would end before Malcolm could get to the heart of whatever existential nightmare had gripped him that moment. It wasn't enough.

He looked down at his very normal breakfast and noticed that he had been vigorously playing with it instead of eating. Maybe three cups of coffee was too much? Malcolm poured himself a shot of whiskey to counter balance the caffeine.

Originally, before the calls began, Mr. Steadman wanted to talk to some sort of councilor or therapist. A professional trained to deal with someone's problems would had been ideal, but a professional of *any* kind was expensive. As far as Malcolm was concerned, mental health services was the domain for a more wealthy class, and it certainly was not something he could ever afford. There was a reason that a higher percentage of the homeless was schizophrenic or bipolar. The ever looming threat of loosing his house was getting closer, would Malcolm join them?

No, of course not, if Malcolm Steadman was going to be a homeless man, he was going to be a normal homeless man.

The customer service hotline was a concession. He figured then that he could call them up, explain his terrifying anxieties and grizzly epiphanies, get some sort of catharsis, and be able to go about the rest of his day normally. For a time, it worked. He felt better afterwards, and no matter how intense or existentially stark his panic attacks, he knew that a simple phone call would set him right. For a few weeks, Malcolm Steadman was able to find a job, go out on a (terribly failed) date, and mingle with co-workers. Then they started hanging up. Everything got far worse.

Without his "fix", everything in his life spiraled out of control, and he was utterly consumed by his existential terrors. Without someone to talk to, Malcolm's days became the same nightmare put on repeat. He would wake up, eat breakfast, have a panic attack that would tear at the foundations of his very reality and being, drink, and assemble the same exact jigsaw puzzle until he either passed out from exhaustion or from the drinking. God. Damn. It. Malcolm Steadman was not normal. This is not what normal people do. This is what only the either incredibly mad did, or what a modern artist did with a camera rolling. Malcolm Steadman did not have it in him to bullshit like a modern artist.

He needed to talk to someone. He left the rest of his eggs on the table as he began to pace. He needed to call someone. He needed a fix.

Then, Malcolm Steadman had an idea.

There was someone he could call, someone who would not charge him, who was a trained professional, and someone who absolutely could not hang up on him for any reason: the Suicide Prevention Hotline.

Malcolm was thinking clearly!

Malcolm's day suddenly got brighter. He could call the suicide hotline, bitch about everything that was troubling him, and get the sort of catharsis and validation he needed. He would not only get his fix, but he would also get some socialization before looking for a job! After he was sober, of course. Malcolm did not want to do anything rash.

Malcolm did not want to do anything he would regret.

Finding the number took him no time. A quick search on his phone's browser and he was instantly pointed in the right direction. He tapped the number and eagerly waited as his phone made a connection. Malcolm got an endorphin rush when the connection was made and he heard the familiar muted cacophony of voices and phones ringing that made up the constant background of a call center. Pavlov would have never imagined this scenario.

Malcolm was chipper. The operator asked for Malcolm's address first, and seemed taken aback that Malcolm answered so quickly. This was not Malcolm's first rodeo. "How can I help you sir?" a soft melodic voice asked Malcolm. The owner of that voice was not prepared for the consequences of that question.

Malcolm Steadman spent the next ten minutes detailing fourth dimensional shadow puppetry to the operator, only being interrupted once to explain what a tesseract was. Malcolm had not been this animate in months, he paced back and forth, laughed heartily, and occasionally lapped up a fork full of eggs and pulled back a shot of whiskey. With his rant about the fourth dimension coming to a close, Malcolm described to the operator how tragic and absurd it was that Malcolm's sad and meaningless life could just be a way for fourth dimensional beings to pass time.

"Do you think your life is meaningless?" The operator asked.

"Oh of course it is meaningless!" Malcolm replied, "That was like the very first epiphany I had!" he continued. To anyone else, Malcolm's lighthearted reminiscing might sound manic.

The details of burnt toast and the whole potential energy of the universe wasted on the permanence of reality television broadcast into the great abyss spewed out of Malcolm quicker than the operator could parse.

"...And that" said Malcolm, "is the, the fucking tragedy of carbon!"

"Have you been drinking?" The operator asked.

"Jus' a 'lil.." Malcolm replied. His next shot he poured in a fresh cup of coffee. He didn't want to get too drunk.

Nostalgia, and how it's opiate effects had lulled him from thinking forward was described to the operator in full. The depressant effects of alcohol had finally mellowed Malcolm, and to anyone else his sudden drop in mood might sound like a despondent depression. If Malcolm wasn't so normal, he would come off as being bi-polar.

"Are you depressed sir?" said the operator.

"Check 'an mate!" a drunk Malcolm responded.

"Do you ever think about ending your life?" asked the operator.

"I think 'bout the end all of the time!" Malcolm replied, preparing the story about his unplugged toaster and the immanency of entropy in his mind. Before he could relate the anecdote, the operator stated: "We don't want you doing anything rash. We do not wanting you doing anything you would regret sir".

Malcolm felt embarrassed. Had the operator sensed his intentions? Malcolm was clearly drunk now, going out looking for work was no longer a sensible thing to do. Malcolm was a normal, responsible man, he would wait until he was sober before looking for a job, that was certain.

"Listen, listen.." Malcolm said, almost whispering, "you don' have ta worry 'bout me okay? I'll do it in the afternoon".

The pause on the other end of the phone was tense. The operator broke the silence now with urgency. "Sir!" the operator said, "I can send you some help".

Malcolm hung up. Panic blossomed in Malcolm's mind like roses on a sped up time-lapse. Help?

Malcolm made a mistake. Malcolm made a BIG mistake. *For some reason,* Malcolm thought in a drunken haze, *that man thinks I'm going to kill myself.* The terror he felt was familiar, though for the first time in three months it was not attributed to something abstract. No, there were real consequences to what Malcolm had done.

No no, he thought, *everything will be okay, it was just a phone call.* Malcolm replayed the mad conversation in his inebriated mind. The first thing that the operator had asked for was his address. The first thing that the operator asked for was how to find him. Malcolm sat down, he tried to calm himself.

A moment passed, then another. Malcolm sat in his kitchen chair and stared at his now cold breakfast. He breathed slowly, trying his best not to give in to his panic attack. A long moment passed.

Then the sirens came.

Distant at first, the high-pitched klaxon of an emergency vehicle grew in tone and volume. Malcolm froze.

The glare of the sun coming through Malcolm's kitchen window was now overwhelmed by an alternating light of red and blue. A moment passed, Malcolm did not move. He watched as two Emergency Medical Technicians and two police officers approached his apartment building. Malcolm suddenly rose to his feet. His apartment was a mess.

A hefty knock shook Malcolm's apartment door and a husky voice yelled his name, saying "can we come in? We are here to help". Malcolm quickly tidied his apartment and answered the door. The conversation was polite, and to the point. Malcolm Steadman was deemed a danger to himself, and it was best if he came with them. Everything was going to be fine.

Malcolm Steadman did not protest, it was simply not in his nature. Malcolm is a normal, average everyman. He is polite and he is a model citizen. He did what he was told. He was led to an ambulance, and he was taken to a hospital for observation.

Malcolm Steadman will become homeless in 90 days.

Continue the countdown with Season Two!

m.p. fitzgerald
existential TERROR and breakfast
season two

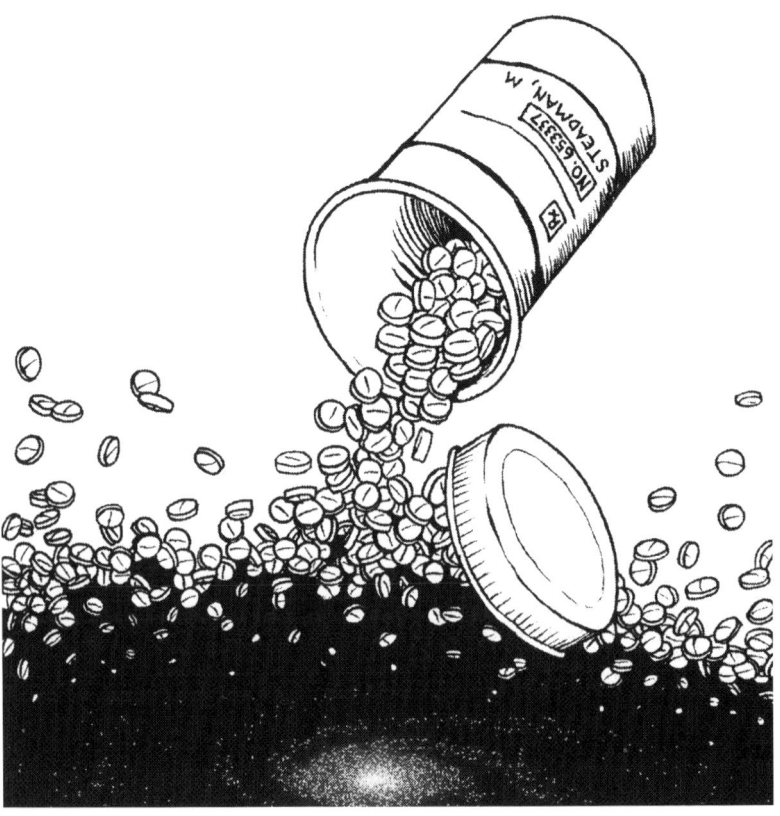

Sign up for the alerts and get the Nihilist's Horoscope *FOR FREE!*

Get The Nihilist's Horoscope!

Tired of all of that hope and positivity in your horoscopes? We all know there is no future. So get some nihilism in your horoscopes, it's like chocolate and peanut butter... Only bleak, irreverent, and funny.

GET THE NIHILIST'S HOROSCOPE FOR FREE:
https://revfitz.com/nihilist/

About the Author:

M.P. Fitzgerald lives in Seattle and is dedicated to injecting the feverish Gonzo style into fiction. He is an author, illustrator, and an amateur mad scientist.

The author greatly appreciates you taking the time to read his work. Please consider leaving a review wherever you bought the book, or telling your friends about it, to help him spread the word.

You can sign up for his newsletter (and get a free book in the process) at: https://revfitz.com/nihilist/

Connect with M.P. Fitzgerald
Website: https://revfitz.com
Email: contact@revfitz.com

Printed in Great Britain
by Amazon